I0773360

Cutler's Cases

a collection of
John Cutler short stories

by Colin Conway

Cutler's Cases: a collection of John Cutler short stories

Cover Design by Zach McCain

ISBN: 979-8-9859409-4-7

Original Ink Press, an imprint of High Speed Creative, LLC
1521 N. Argonne Road, #C-205
Spokane Valley, WA 99212

Visit the author's website at www.colinconway.com

Contents

Introduction

My writing career began in 1996. Sometime during that year, I sat at my computer and wrote a single-page story. It featured a cop drinking in a bar. Anger and bluster filled every word. It was an unreadable tale written by an unhappy man.

At that time, I didn't know that I would soon be a police officer. That was still three years into the future, and I hadn't even imagined such a thing possible. I was simply a guy whose world had crumbled around him. The company I worked for sold, and I was soon out of a job. My marriage ended that same week—we only had to file the paperwork to make it official. And the dog we'd recently adopted ran away.

For one week, my life turned into a clichéd country song.

I didn't know how to deal with the feelings surrounding those events. My friends weren't the type I could share those emotions with. I didn't journal, and seeing a counselor never crossed my mind. Therefore, the sentiments about my situation remained bottled up. The pressure built, and it needed a place to escape.

***

While in the Army, I noodled around with a couple of short stories. They weren't anything special—basically, a guy experimenting with ideas. In college, I wrote a few pieces for various English classes. Again, nothing extraordinary—just some assignments, but I was proud of them. My friends and family read them and said the kind of things that those types are apt to say, "That's nice," or "I didn't know you could write."

I carried an idea in my heart that someday I would be a writer. I'd been telling it to myself since I was in junior high school. I had an English teacher who once said my writing style reminded her of Ernest Hemingway. I didn't understand it then, and I don't see the comparison today, but I got that she meant it as a compliment. I puffed with pride.

In high school, I shared the lofty dream of being an author, and some family members playfully asked when I would write the next great American novel. I had no idea who wrote the first great American novel, if there might have been a second, and how I could fit into that lineage. I stopped talking about being a writer after that. I didn't want to be mocked any further.

Those teasing questions lingered into my twenties.

***

With a divorce looming and negative emotions building, I turned on my computer one evening and wrote, "Motherfucker."

I don't know why I wrote that expletive, but I didn't have anything else in my head except that single word. I wanted to scream it from the roof of my house. I wanted to shake my fist at God for how things had gone wrong in my life. It wasn't supposed to have turned out this way. But I didn't do those things.

Standing on the roof would make me a maniac—that's what society said.

Shaking my fist at God might send me to hell—that's what the church had taught me.

But writing "motherfucker" on that page felt good.

The single-page story finished itself quickly. As I

mentioned at the start of the introduction, it was terrible. But a bit of steam escaped. Some pressure was relieved.

That short story led to a second which was then followed by a decade of quick tales—easily more than a hundred, possibly two. I've never spent the time to count. So many are bad that I've considered deleting them to remove them from existence. However, I don't get rid of them because I want the reminder of my journey—of where I started, how I got here, and how painful the road was. Those stories are my journal.

Unfortunately, what they revealed was how unhappy I was.

Most of the tales were dark or sad, and they had unlikable protagonists filled with ugly flaws. I didn't like the lead characters in most of the stories.

That should have been expected as I didn't like myself then.

***

I wrote the first John Cutler novel in 2004.

That book was called *Running in Circles*, and Cutler was known by a different name—Jack Collins. Two more novels quickly followed—one in 2005 (*Dog Town*) and another in 2006 (*Sticks and Stones*). I was proud of those books, yet I shouldn't have been.

My pride was based solely on the fact that I wrote a book. That seemed a significant achievement when compared to a short story, but quality should dictate self-esteem, not quantity. I should have been proud that I wrote a good book—not that I managed to string together 65,000 words.

I couldn't see any glaring issues with those books, yet there were plenty—the primary of which was Jack. He wasn't someone most readers would want to spend time with. He was angry, misogynistic, and lost. A more accomplished writer might have been able to pull off that feat, but I couldn't.

Jack Collins was a one-dimensional bore. He complained about everything, fought without provocation, and swore too much. He was everything I thought a tough-guy private investigator was supposed to be.

Worse, he didn't grow over the three books. He remained an immature man-child.

Whenever Jack couldn't get to the heart of a problem, he slugged someone for the truth. And if that didn't work, he waved his gun like a lunatic. By the time I wrote those books, I'd been a cop, and I should have known better. But I parroted what I read in action books and what I saw in the movies. However, I wasn't copying the good stuff, only the bad.

"Me, tough guy. You talk or else."

***

Strangely, there was enough in that first Jack Collins manuscript to interest a young agent. She signed me up and shopped around *Running in Circles*. Luckily, no one picked it up. However, I didn't think I was fortunate at the time. Instead, I felt discouraged and heartbroken.

Looking back, I dodged the proverbial bullet. Nobody accepting *Running in Circles* was a gift as it allowed Jack Collins to sit for seventeen years.

The manuscript seasoned, and I matured both as a writer and as a man.

***

He might have been seasoning, but Jack Collins didn't sit idly. I pulled out the manuscript and flipped it over in its marinade now and then. At first, my editing attempts were half-hearted because I thought the books were done. I thought I'd nailed that first story, and I still couldn't see the flaws in the character.

But each time I came back to that *Running in Circles* manuscript, the more I hated it. I began to despise Jack as well. That didn't mean I wanted to throw away all that work. The skeleton of the story had merit, and parts of Jack did, too. The problem was I didn't know which parts to keep and which to jettison.

There's advice in the writing field that says authors must kill their darlings. It means they need to get rid of anything self-indulgent or anything that they hold precious in their manuscripts. Eventually, I realized Jack was my darling, and he was holding me back.

As you can see, Jack Collins embodied a lot of me at the time. He was angry that his marriage had fallen apart, and he was mad about leaving the police department. In general, he was an unhappy person.

Here's a not-so-fun fact. During that time, I told people I needed to be angry to write. How messed up is that?

My solution came from reading a James Lee Burke novel. One of Burke's more famous creations is a serial murderer named Preacher Jack Collins. Imagine my surprise when I read that. I couldn't have my hero named the same as Preacher Jack Collins. Maybe I could, but this finally nudged me to kill my darling.

It didn't hurt that I was finally happy in my life. I wanted the character to be reborn.

***

Creating John Cutler allowed me to rewrite the entire Jack Collins back story.

Cutler would be a man who could learn and grow (a constant theme in my writings now), but I removed the failing marriage he was so upset about. Instead, I gave him a daughter from a short-term relationship. This allowed him to feel guilt and struggle to connect, but it removed a huge chunk of his anger.

I removed the resentment for the police department. He disliked certain officers, but Cutler could see his part in his downfall. He wasn't so myopic like his earlier incarnation.

As the series progresses, Cutler still punches his way to answers, but he's less of a wild card now. If you read these books and decide that he still is, imagine him worse—way worse.

Those three Jack Collins novels were eventually reborn as *Cutler's Return*, *Cutler's Chase*, and *Cutler's Friend*. I'm proud of those stories now. It took a lot of work to mold them into something different, and I'm happy to see them on a shelf next to my other series.

I'm also excited about Cutler's future. The first novel starts in 2004. I figure I've got a lot of writing to get Cutler up to modern day.

***

What you're about to read now are five short stories. Four of them were written when I drafted the original three novels. The fifth story was written in 2022 as a needed backstory for a character.

The four original short stories went through the same maturation process as the books. One made an appearance in a short story collection. However, they've all gone through significant rewrites since then as the character was reborn. If you're interested in how the short stories came about, I'll share some information about them at the end of the book.

I hope you enjoy Cutler's journey as much as I did writing it.

Colin Conway
Spring 2022

Every day, no matter how you fight it,
you learn a little more about yourself,
and all most of it does is teach humility.

– John D. MacDonald/
One Fearful Yellow Eye

Cutler's Cases

Manny

Manny Gorman clenched his fists and bared his teeth. A man acting like a crazed grizzly is a scary sight, especially when he stands six and a half feet tall and weighs three hundred pounds. Manny and I had fought for nearly ninety seconds which is a lifetime when throwing and taking punches. His face was bloodied. I imagined mine was more so.

We destroyed Manny's living room in the process of our brawl. Once bright lamps were now shattered. Pictures lay on the ground with their frames busted. A crack ran through the middle of his TV.

Yet Manny remained on his feet, ready for more. The time to talk myself free from his violence had long passed.

The big man had come home early. He was supposed to be out drinking with his brother. "Letting off some steam," according to his wife. Instead, he found me on the couch with her. Seeing Delores in my arms, Manny went crazy.

It would have been better for her to come to my place. Hindsight is a worthless thing in moments like this.

I punched Manny in the nose—the third time I'd done so. Unlike the others, this one barely staggered him. His eyes had stopped watering by now. He did, however, bring his hands closer to his face as he shook off the blow.

My window to win this fight was razor-thin, and I had no illusions about that. To survive the night—to survive Manny Gorman—I needed to get by him and escape the house. That was my only option.

Moving quickly, I grabbed Manny's shoulders and jerked a knee into his groin. He grunted and reflexively snapped forward. Men respond in a predictable manner when struck in the testicles, but fights are messy, and they get uglier the longer they go on.

Manny's head smashed into mine—an inadvertent strike caused by my leg thrusting into his groin. I stumbled backward. The room spun wickedly, and I reached out for anything to stop my fall. My legs buckled, and I grabbed onto the edge of a leather recliner—his favorite chair.

Delores shrieked as Manny advanced.

He jumped and tackled me—a linebacker punishing an unprotected punter. His considerable weight pinned me to the floor.

Disoriented now, I frantically wriggled to get free. Panic welled inside me.

Manny yelled, "My wife!"

He punched me in the cheek. A second strike swung in an arc and missed me entirely. This seemed to anger him further. He pounded straight down onto my chest—it felt like a jackhammer trying to reach my spine.

Manny fell forward until his face was inches from mine. His fingers slipped into my hair.

I wanted to holler, but there was no breath to do so.

"This'll teach you," he said. Spittle flew from his lips.

When my head bounced off the floor, the lights flicked off.

***

Manny Gorman kept a secret from his wife, and Delores thought it was another woman.

She'd noticed little things like contradictions in his

statements and changes in behavior. Then he snuck out after she went to sleep. Not once, but twice. She didn't confront him, but she worried about it—a lot. Things finally came to a head when Manny called in late to work.

Manny wasn't the type of man to miss any time. He took pride in his work ethic.

When she finally decided to act, Delores came by my office. I want to say she picked me because of my reputation or a friendly referral, but proximity was her deciding factor. My office was three blocks from her West Central home, and she didn't have a car.

Delores Gorman was a slight woman. She wore a printed cotton dress that was threadbare near the shoulders. A black headband held her salt and pepper hair away from her face. Errant strands poked free and drooped down her forehead. Other than muted red lipstick, she didn't wear any make-up.

She lowered her gaze when she said, "He's got a woman."

"How do you know?"

"I know."

"Have you talked to him about it?"

Her eyes met mine. "You don't talk to Manny about something like that."

"Why not?"

She shook her head. "It's not done."

"Delores, are you afraid of your husband?"

The woman studied her hands.

"Does Manny hit you?"

Delores jerked her head up. "Never." She appeared offended that I dared ask such a thing. "He's not that kind of man."

"Then why are you afraid?"

Her lips momentarily pinched together and then

released. There was a slight tremor in the lower one. "What if he leaves?"

I cocked my head.

"Look at me, Mr. Cutler. Manny and I are the same age, but he's still handsome and desirable. And me…"

It was a silly concern, but one that I couldn't assuage at that moment.

I rested my elbows on my desk. "What happens if it's true?"

Delores sighed. Before answering, she looked away. "I only want to know."

"Maybe not knowing is better."

She shook her head again, but this time, she avoided eye contact. "Not knowing is harder."

I did my best to talk her out of it, but in the end, we agreed on a rate for my services.

***

The next morning, I dropped by the site where Manny Gorman currently worked.

Sonnen Development was gutting a century-old three-story building in the heart of downtown. *Condominiums Available* read a banner hanging down from the edge of the roof.

I didn't see Manny, so I walked into the nearby Satellite Diner and slid into a booth next to the window. The location gave me a view of the site and allowed me to enjoy a plate of hash browns.

Around eight, Manny wandered by my window. He was easy to spot because he looked exactly like the picture that Delores brought the day we met. Manny was big and stocky. His clothes consisted of a red flannel shirt as a jacket, a black t-shirt underneath, faded blue jeans, tan boots, and a Jack Daniels baseball cap. According to

Delores, that was his standard work outfit. Even among construction workers, Manny Gorman was hard to miss.

Delores referred to her husband as handsome and desirable. Men are lucky that their women see them differently than the rest of the world because Manny was neither handsome nor desirable. He had the hard, thick face of a warrior. His body was built to fight in the gladiator matches of old. Not the oiled-up musclebound movies of modern times, but the gruesome ugliness of our ancestors. Plain and simple, Manny Gorman was a bruiser, and he found work that suited him.

For a couple of hours, I watched him work. He lugged heavy equipment about. He swung a sledgehammer to break free a portion of concrete. He hefted tarps onto the back of a truck.

Near ten o'clock, the demolition crew took a break. Manny checked his watch before trotting across the street. For a moment, I thought he might walk into the diner. Once he made the sidewalk, he continued east.

I stood and pulled out a handful of bills to cover my tab.

"Thanks for the browns," I said to my server and left the diner. On the sidewalk, I caught a glimpse of Manny turning the corner.

I jogged to the end of the block, but by the time I got there, he was gone. Manny Gorman had disappeared.

Traffic zoomed northbound on Washington.

Figuring he had to come back this way, I leaned against a brick wall and waited. It seemed too early for Manny's lunch. He'd only been on shift for a couple of hours. This should only be a quick break.

My gaze swiveled from where he'd gone back to the job site. I didn't want to be so focused on where he headed, only to have him return from another direction. My head continued to rotate left and right.

A glass door opened further up the sidewalk, and Manny stepped out. He checked his watch then hurried toward me. I averted my gaze and pretended to be interested in my shoes.

Manny jogged by then turned the corner. He continued his trot all the way back to the job site. When he arrived, he picked up a sledgehammer and reentered the building.

I headed up the street to find the business Manny had just exited.

The logo in the window read *Sam's Computer Haven*. It was a little shop that advertised repairs for all brands. I pushed open the glass door and entered. Grating techno music pumped through the speakers that hung in the corners of the store.

Various used and rebuilt computers lined several shelves with hand-written price tags taped to their cases. A layer of dust covered everything in the place. The shop smelled of body odor and mildew. If failure had an aroma, I imagined it might be like this.

A low moan emanated from behind the counter. I leaned over it to find a twenty-something with blue hair sitting on the floor. He held a hand over one eye as he continued to mew.

"You all right?" I asked.

The guy started at my voice and a single eye widened.

"Manny do that to you?"

The guy stood and dropped his hand away from his face. The skin around his eye was red and swollen. "I'm closed."

"Why did Manny hit you?"

The guy pointed at the door. "Please go."

I rested my hands on the counter. "C'mon, man. What happened?"

"Are you picking up or dropping off?"

"Neither. I only want to know—"

"I'm closed." He covered his eye again and walked into the back.

"I get it," I said and left the store.

Back at the Satellite Diner, I grabbed another seat that gave me a view of the construction site. My previous server cocked her head when she saw me.

"Back so soon?"

"Still hungry, I guess."

She brought me a new glass of water and another menu.

When the construction crew finally broke for lunch, I was on my third glass of water and second piece of apple pie.

A black Lexus pulled to the corner, and Manny climbed in. The luxury car entered traffic and soon vanished around the corner.

Did the car belong to Manny's girlfriend? If so, what would a woman who drove a car like that want with a low-rent guy like Manny? Maybe she was the type of woman who got off on the gladiators.

Three members of the demolition crew sauntered down the street and entered Chicken-N-Mo.

Nothing exciting was going to happen during the lunch break, especially with Manny gone. A change of locale might do me good, and maybe I could induce a conversation with the three and learn something about Manny.

By the time I made it to the small restaurant, the men had already ordered and gotten a table.

A young black woman stood ready with a pen and notepad when I approached the counter.

"A side of coleslaw and a water," I said.

Her brow furrowed. "That's it?"

"I'm not very hungry."

She shrugged and turned to fill my order.

I sat at the table next to the members of the construction crew. I glanced surreptitiously at them every now and then.

The three I followed were chubby, skinny, and old. Therefore, I nicknamed them Roly Poly, Bean Pole, and Wrinkles. I never professed to be clever with nicknames. While they ate, the three told stories and laughed.

When I finally worked up the courage to ask them about Manny Gorman, the big man walked into the little restaurant. The three men stopped talking and watched him the way sheep eye an approaching coyote.

Manny ordered two pieces of chicken to-go. While the cook prepared his order, the big man faced his co-workers.

"Hey, fellas," Manny said.

They all smiled and nodded, but no one said a word.

After Manny paid for his order, he strolled out of the restaurant, still without a word from the others.

The chatter at the nearby table heated up again.

"You believe that guy?" Wrinkles asked.

"Mister Untouchable now." Bean Pole air-quoted 'Mister Untouchable.'

Roly Poly wiped his lips with the back of his hand. "That's what happens when you start playing in that rarified air. He's got more important things to do than talk with us humps."

Rarified air, I thought. Were they jealous of Manny's girlfriend?

Wrinkles caught me observing them. "You listening to our conversation, friend?"

I pointed at what remained of my coleslaw. "Just eating."

"Don't let us stop you."

The three of them stopped talking and watched me then.

It was time for me to leave.

***

I wanted a new vantage point to surveil the construction site, and I found it in the ironically named Soup Kitchen, a restaurant specializing in its namesake. The menu prices weren't for the disenfranchised.

When the server arrived at my table near the window, I ordered a cup of black coffee. She fought back a frown before bringing me a cup. She didn't ask if I wanted to order anything else.

The seat provided a perfect spot to watch the construction site. Time passed slower than I could have imagined. While waiting, I ate small bowls of potato soup, cheddar broccoli soup, and chicken noodle. Eating was the cost of renting the seat for four hours. I felt bloated and sluggish with a belly full of soup.

After the second bowl, the server politely asked me to settle up.

"You don't have to leave, but I'm closing out." Her smile was apologetic. "I hope you understand."

"I do." It was downtown. I'm sure they'd seen a dine and dash before.

She approvingly eyed the cash I pulled from my pocket. I satisfied the bill and tipped her.

"I'm meeting a friend," I said. "They're not going to be here for a couple more hours. Hope you don't mind."

"If we need the table, I'll let you know."

Hence, the bowl of chicken noodle.

Manny ended the workday without ever leaving the job site again. When it was time to pack it in, he strolled in my general direction. He was on the opposite side of the street from Soup Kitchen, so I didn't move.

He stepped into the mouth of an alley and casually leaned a shoulder against a wall. His gaze swept past the restaurant as he surveyed the street.

Did he know I was watching?

In hopes of moving away from the window, I leaned back into my chair. I felt exposed, but I didn't want to leave Soup Kitchen to change my position. Going out front meant revealing my position. Slinking out the back meant losing visual contact with the man.

Instead, I sat still and watched.

Nothing happened for several minutes. Manny simply gazed up and down the street—a man killing time.

A woman walked up to him. She wore an oversized sweatshirt and baggy sweatpants. They exchanged a few perfunctory words before Manny scowled at her. The woman bowed her head and nodded.

I pulled a digital camera from my jacket and did my best to shield it from the few customers in the establishment.

Across the street, the strange interaction continued. The woman handed Manny something. He opened his hand and flipped through a wad of bills. When the big man finished counting, he shoved the money into his pocket. He never gave the woman anything. He simply said something and returned to leaning on the wall. She headed back in the direction she came.

For the next fifteen minutes, Manny barely moved. But inside the restaurant, I fidgeted in my chair.

A young black man approached Manny. He gesticulated while he spoke. From his body language, it appeared the man was trying to apologize to Manny but doing a poor job of it.

Manny pushed off the wall and stuck an accusatory finger out. This backed the young man up, and he lifted his hands in protection. Manny slapped away the man's hands and punched him in the stomach. The young man dropped to his knees and cradled his belly. Manny stood over him and said a few words.

The younger man quickly dug into his pocket, pulled something out, and held it above his head. Manny stepped back and counted a wad of bills. When he was satisfied, he headed northbound.

I pulled several bills from my pocket and tossed them on the table. "Thank you," I called to the server. She waved back as I bolted from the restaurant.

In the mouth of the alley, the young man now sat with his back against the same wall Manny had been using.

I squatted and asked, "Are you okay?"

The man eyed me with distrust.

"Why'd Manny hit you?"

"Leave it alone." The man worked himself to his feet. He held onto the wall with one hand and his stomach with the other.

"Who's Manny working for?"

A smirk crossed the kid's face. "If you don't know, count yourself lucky." He brushed past me as he walked away.

I headed deeper into the alley and let my mind drift over the day. It didn't take a genius to figure out what Manny was doing. He was a blue-collar tough guy who assaulted two people during the day, and neither seemed interested in talking about it. He was handling wads of money and sneaking around at night. Manny Gorman wasn't messing around with a woman—I knew that now—but he wanted to keep his wife from knowing what he was up to.

A black luxury car turned into the far end of the alley. Behind me, an engine gunned. I glanced over my shoulder. A pick-up blocked the opposite end, preventing any possible escape.

I stopped walking. There was nowhere for me to go, and my gun was safely at home. There was nothing to do but wait.

The Lexus continued toward me and stopped a few feet away. Besides the driver, it appeared someone sat in the middle of the back seat.

A tall man with broad shoulders and a reddish afro climbed from the front. He made a show of extending to his full height before pulling his shoulders back. The guy might have played forward for a college basketball team. He smirked then opened the rear door. That movement revealed a gun tucked into the back of his pants.

A much shorter man emerged from the car. He wore a rust-colored t-shirt, black jeans, and black cowboy boots. At best, he stood five-seven. His dark hair was styled short in a businessman's cut, and he had a neatly trimmed beard that gave him the look of a constant five o'clock shadow.

The smaller man walked toward me. He had judging eyes and a curl to his upper lip. Behind him, the driver moved in step, throwing his shoulders like a boxer walking into the ring.

"Who are you?" the cowboy asked.

It seemed an excellent time for the truth. "John Cutler."

"You a cop?"

I used to be, but I didn't think saying so would help matters. "No."

The driver said, "Smells like one."

"See?" the cowboy said. "Everyone thinks you are."

I shrugged. "What can I say?"

The boss punched me in the stomach. It was a sloppy strike that he telegraphed by widening his eyes and winding up. I took it, though, and it hurt. What other choice was there? A gun was involved in this confrontation, and it wasn't mine.

"What's your game, Cutler?"

"I'm not playing—"

The smaller man kicked me in the shin. I hadn't expected that, and the toe of his cowboy boots hurt much worse than his fist. I hopped and held my leg.

"Knock off the lies," the little cowboy said. "We got business to discuss."

I dropped my leg and reset my stance. My shin hurt like hell, and my stomach ached, but none of it was as bad as the damage done to my pride. If he pulled that stunt again, I wasn't going to stand for it.

"Seems we're having trouble communicating," the shorter man said.

"Seems," I agreed.

"Why were you following Manny?"

"Who's Manny?"

The boss punched, but I weaved. Then I countered and caught him in the mouth. The cowboy stumbled into the driver. As the tall man caught his boss, I was on them both.

The driver couldn't get free and risk dropping his employer. Courtesy dictated so. This allowed me to reach behind the driver's back and yank the gun free from his pants.

As the cowboy regained his footing, he said, "Take it easy, tough guy."

The driver's eyes widened, and his hands went into the air.

Down the alley, two men exited the rig that blocked that escape route. They ran toward us now.

"Call them off," I said.

The cowboy raised his hand, and the two men slowed.

I studied the shorter man. "You have me at a disadvantage."

"You're the one with the gun."

"You know my name, but I don't know yours."

A trickle of blood ran from the corner of the cowboy's mouth. He dabbed at the blood with a finger, glanced at it with some curiosity, then returned his gaze to me. "Milo."

"And him?"

"He doesn't matter. Not since you got his gun." Milo eyed his driver. "That's your gun, isn't it?"

"Yeah, but—"

Milo lifted a hand, and the driver stopped talking.

I said, "What's Manny gotten into?"

The smaller man removed a handkerchief from his inside jacket pocket and wiped his fingers with it, but his eyes never left me. "You want something? Then I want something."

"You want to know why I'm following Manny."

Milo nodded. "Tit for tat."

"His wife is worried."

The smaller man stared blankly.

"About another woman."

Milo burst into laughter. The driver joined in, but the boss turned and eyed him into silence. "You don't get to do that. Not after what happened."

"But boss—"

"Don't do that." Milo faced me. "This whole thing you're doing is because of Manny's woman?"

I nodded.

Milo tucked his handkerchief away. "And you aren't a cop?"

"Private investigator."

"That smells right." Milo nodded. "Okay, fine. Manny's working off a debt."

"Dope or cards?"

"Neither. The big boy took out a loan that he's working off in exchange. I don't know what for, and I don't care, but he's in my employ until we're even."

"And he collects for you?"

Milo shrugged. "Among other things."

"Like what?"

"That's none of your concern. I told you what you need to know to calm the wife and earn your fee. But a word to the wise, Cutler. Manny has a short fuse. Don't piss him off." He jerked his head toward his car. "We're going now. I believe both of our worries have been addressed. Can my man have his gun back?"

I ejected the round but didn't bother catching it. Then I pressed the release button and let the magazine clatter to the ground.

The driver stepped menacingly forward. "I'm gonna bust you in the mouth."

Milo held up a hand. "You'll do nothing of the sort."

I extended the empty gun to the cowboy, and he took it.

"Good day, Cutler."

Milo waved to the men at the opposite end of the alley, and the truck backed around the corner.

I turned and walked away.

***

Later that night, I sat in Delores Gorman's living room. Manny, she told me, was out with his brother drinking at the Maxwell House, a local bar.

The Gormans lived in a small two-bedroom home that they rented. Their furniture was out-of-style and worn, but the house was clean and well-kept. An old television with fat knobs sat inside a dated home entertainment center. Delores and I shared the couch as we talked.

"He's not seeing another woman, Delores."

"You're sure?"

"I'm positive."

She sighed in relief then closed her eyes. It took me a moment to realize she was praying. When she finished, Delores opened her eyes. "If there's no woman, then what's he been doing at those strange hours? And why's he so irritable lately?"

I laid it out. She paid for the truth, and I didn't hide any of it. When I was done talking, Delores put her hands over her face and cried.

"He's a big man, Delores. I'm sure he can take care of himself."

She dropped her hands and shook her head. "You don't understand. He came home a few weeks ago with ten thousand dollars. He said it was a loan from his boss. We needed that money as a down payment to get my mother into a nursing home. No bank would loan it to us, but Manny came home with it like he promised he would."

Delores burst into tears again, and her body shook. I wrapped my arm around her and tried my best to comfort her. The little words I whispered were of little consolation.

The front door swung open, and Manny Gorman stepped into his home. The smile he wore dropped immediately, and redness blossomed across his cheeks. "The hell?"

"Manny," Delores said through tear-filled eyes.

I stood to explain my presence and only succeeded in looking guilty. He crossed the room like a heat-seeking missile. Manny knocked my hands out of the way and pinned me to the sofa. The fight was on, and I started in a losing position.

It only got worse from there.

Ninety seconds passed before Manny sat on top of me. He held my hair in his huge hands.

That's when the lights went out.

***

When reality returned, the first thing I saw was Manny.

I lazily punched him in the forehead. He swatted my hand away.

"Hey," Manny said, "knock it off before you hurt yourself."

I struggled to get up, but Manny held me down.

Delores appeared over his shoulder then. "It's okay, John. Everything is okay."

Her voice was soft, and I lay back, shutting my eyes.

***

When I awoke next, I was on the sofa with an ice pack on my face. I sat up slowly and wanted to retch. The ice pack fell into my lap.

Delores moved next to me, and Manny leaned forward in a nearby chair. Worry creased his face.

"It's okay," Delores whispered.

Manny said, "I didn't mean to hurt you."

"You didn't?" It seemed the most foolish thing a man had ever said.

Delores patted my hand. "He was upset at seeing us together." She seemed pleasantly happy at the turn of events. "I explained everything to Manny."

His brow furrowed. "Why didn't you come up and ask me what I was doing?"

I stared at him. "Are you serious?"

Manny shrugged. "I'm not a bad man."

The pain in my entire body disagreed with him. I stood shakily.

"Where are you going?" Manny asked.

"Home."

"I'll help you." He stepped over and held me up by the arm. "I promise." His voice was oddly comforting.

Delores smiled. "Thank you for your help, John. I'm sorry for how it turned out, but— thank you, anyway."

I nodded once then let the big man escort me outside. We headed toward my place. We'd only walked by a couple of houses before Manny apologized again.

"You're not like I imagined," I said.

"How's that?"

"I watched you smack around a couple people today."

"You saw that?" Manny frowned. "They owed money and wouldn't pay."

"So, they got beat?"

"Those are the terms. Don't borrow if you can't pay it back."

"Like you?"

The frown never left Manny's face. "That's right. I don't like hurtin' people, but I do it because I needed the money for Delores' mom."

"Your wife loves you," I told him. The ground tilted slowly to the left, and I tried to blink it back to level.

Manny held tighter to my arm. "I got worried when I saw her with you."

"How long do you have to work for Milo before you're paid off?"

"Not sure, but Milo will treat me fair."

I stopped in front of my place. The world swayed, so I grabbed onto a nearby tree. "You trust him?"

"I may not be a smart man, John, but I don't take too well to being treated poorly. Milo knows that."

"I'm sure he does."

Manny dug into his back pocket and pulled out an envelope. "Delores said to give this to you."

"What is it?"

"Your fee."

I stared at Manny.

"You did work for her, and you earned it. We pay all our debts."

I wanted to say something, but nothing came to mind

Manny patted my shoulder. "Have a nice night, John. Sorry about the—" he waved toward my face. "Why don't you come by some night. We'll have a beer."

"I'd like that."

He ambled away. When he was out of sight, I lowered to a knee.

Then I pitched forward and lay in my front yard.

It seemed easier than walking inside.

The Problem with Suzie

The scalding shower eased my muscles but did little to wash away the hangover. Why had I drunk so much? I knew better. Bile rose in my throat, and I struggled to swallow it down. Giving up, I bent over and heaved. Nothing came up, and I felt worse for it.

From the backyard, the dog barked. "Shut up," I yelled and felt stupid for it. Not only was it the wrong command for him to stop, but it hurt my head. Now, everything ached worse. Still bent over, I held my stomach. Water ran around my face and into my eyes and my mouth.

I spat and muttered, "Shit."

There comes a moment in a bad hangover where I might pray to a God that I don't necessarily believe in. It's done with a foolish hope that he'll relieve my pain. I was about to do that when the shower curtain ripped open.

The shock of someone being in the house surprised me, and I jumped away. There was nowhere to go. I banged into the shower wall and lost my footing. Reaching out for something to grab ahold, I found nothing but slickness. I collapsed into the bathtub.

A rail of a man stood in my bathroom. He clutched a gun in his right hand. He wore black slacks and a short-sleeved black shirt. "Get up."

Slowly, I rose to my feet. Tactically, I was at a horrible disadvantage. For starters, he had a gun. Next, he was dressed. And lastly, I stood barefoot on a slick surface. If I wanted to make any move against him, I would have to step over the side of the tub. There wasn't anything to do but cover myself.

The tall man stepped back and motioned with his Glock. "Out."

"Yeah, okay." I turned and twisted the hot and cold faucet dials.

The stranger stepped forward and angrily shoved my shoulder. My feet slipped out from under me, and I crumpled into the tub. My head smacked against the wall.

"I didn't say turn off the water."

The throbbing in my temples increased but the desire to vomit vanished. Carefully, I stood and stepped from the tub. I reached for a towel. "What's this about?"

"Another man's woman." He whipped his gun down, and the barrel smacked across my testicles. I collapsed to the floor. "You think there wouldn't be repercussions?"

I lay on the floor and shuddered.

The tall man squatted next to me, and the gun hung loosely between his legs. "You should have thought ahead."

I lifted my head to protest, but he punched me with his free hand.

The stranger stood then and tucked his gun into his waistband. "Consider this your first warning. There won't be a second." His gaze shifted to my testicles. "You might want to put a towel on that."

I touched my groin then raised a hand. My fingers were covered in blood.

"Stay there," he said.

He left the room then, and I lay my head on the floor.

***

I don't know how much time passed, but I lost track of it because of the pain—it seemed everywhere all at once. My head hurt from not only the hangover but the stranger's punch. My back and hips hurt from the repeated falls. And my hands cupped my throbbing testicles.

Outside, my German Shepherd barked.

I struggled to sit upright. A wave of nausea rolled over me, and I gently scooted to the toilet. The movement hurt in ways I hadn't expected. I finally vomited.

Footsteps pounded from the hallway and into the bathroom. I looked up in time to see the tall man again. I didn't bother cleaning the sick from my lips. Instead, I lowered my hands to protect my loins.

"The man's not here yet," the stranger said calmly.

When he was close enough, he punched down. I fell to the floor but didn't pass out.

The tall man eyed me for a moment. Then he turned and left.

***

I must have given into the pain and fallen asleep. Water splashed on my face and pulled me back from the darkness.

My eyes fluttered open. The stranger stood over me. He held a now-empty cup in his hand.

"Get up."

I rolled to my hands and knees then heaved. My stomach clenched repeatedly, but nothing came.

"Puke on my shoes, and I'll knock holy hell out of you."

I turned away and heaved again. Nothing this time either.

"The man's here. He wants to talk."

Corporal continued to bark from the backyard.

With effort, I rolled back to my knees and the balls of my feet. My groin felt on fire, and I reached down to check it.

The tall man asked, "What's with that dog?"

"It's what he does."

"If he doesn't stop it soon, I'll stop it for him."

The stranger grabbed my hair and yanked me toward the door. I struggled to stand, but he jerked me again. I tried to pry him loose with both of my hands. He clubbed my top hand with the butt of his gun. I let go of him then, and he yanked me once more. I fought to retain my balance until we made it to the kitchen. When he let go, I dropped to the linoleum floor.

Sitting at the kitchen table was a man in his mid-fifties. He had narrow eyes and a bald head. His belly protruded over his belt. The man stared at me with the fascination a child might have right before they rip the wings off a butterfly. "Mr. Cutler?"

I worked myself upright and onto my knees. "And you are?"

He leaned forward. "Do you make a habit of—" He grimaced. "Have you no decency?"

My hands covered my groin.

The fat man raised a single eyebrow. "Do you make a habit of soiling women that don't belong to you?"

"Who are we talking about?"

The tall man in the kitchen corner moved closer; the Glock dangled in his hand.

"Quint," the fat man said softly.

The tall man stopped and eyed his boss.

"Not until I say."

Quint eyed his boss.

"There will be plenty of time for that."

The tall man stepped back to the corner.

I wanted to say plenty of snarky things right then but sitting naked in front of two strangers while my testicles bled doesn't inspire the toughest mindset in a man. I remained silent.

The fat man leaned forward again. "You must be quite the lover if you can't recall your last conquest."

"I'm not in the habit of kissing and telling."

Outside, Corporal continued to bark.

He frowned. "That dog is giving me a headache. Quint, why don't you go outside and silence that thing?"

Quint nodded and turned for the back door.

"Suzie," I said, and Quint stopped. "Her name was Suzie."

The fat man settled back into the chair. "So, you do remember." He rested his arm along the edge of the table. "Even for a man like you, it must have been obvious that she was spoken for."

"She never said."

Quint took a half-step forward then stopped. He appeared anxious to strike me again. The guy seemed to be the type who wanted to fight rather than talk. Had things not been the way they were, I would have happily obliged. He had the kind of face that didn't need a reason to be punched.

The fat man said, "What did she tell you?"

"Nothing."

"Mr. Cutler, don't take me for a fool. A man doesn't bed a woman without some pre-coital conversation. I may not be the most handsome man in the world, but I know a thing or two."

"It was all small talk."

The fat man briefly cocked his head until he arrived at a new question. "Did she share facts about her personal life?"

"Nothing. Everything was shallow."

"That's comforting."

"Not for me."

He smiled now. "Very astute. It seems Suzie has

brought you some trouble."

"I wouldn't have done anything had I known she was with you."

His grin morphed into a smirk. "I highly doubt that. Suzie doesn't take to no very well, and you don't seem the discriminating type."

As the fat man drummed his fingers on the table, he watched them intently. He was considering something, which was most likely what to do with me. I needed some more information before he concluded.

"How did you find out?" I asked.

The fingers stopped their rhythm, but the fat man's attention stayed on his hand. "She bragged about it." His gaze slowly swept to me. "Does that surprise you?"

"Nothing surprises me right now."

He shifted in his chair. "It was Suzie's way of getting even."

"For what?"

The fat man waggled a finger. "You don't get to know that, but I will tell you something. She tried to protect you, Mr. Cutler, but eventually, everyone tells Quint their truths."

I glanced at the tall man in the corner. His face remained flat.

"What should I do with you?" the fat man asked.

"Let me be."

"It was a rhetorical question."

Quint said, "There's no telling what she told him."

The fat man stood. "I agree. Find out what he knows." He turned and left the kitchen. Neither Quint nor I moved until the fat man exited the house.

When the front door closed, I said, "We don't—"

Quint lifted a finger to his lips and pointed his gun at me. "Shh."

Outside, an engine started, and Corporal barked louder.

When the car drove away, the tall man nodded. "Now, we begin."

"You don't have to do this."

"We have to know what she told you."

"I already told you—" I moved one leg from underneath me so I could put a foot solidly on the floor.

"Stay down." Quint stepped closer.

His mistake was built on overconfidence. I was on dry floor now, and I knew the stakes—either I fought or died.

"I'm telling you—" he started.

I jumped and grabbed the barrel of his gun. Quint instinctively yanked it. When that didn't get it free, he pulled the trigger. A round fired and landed somewhere in the kitchen. Due to my hand gripping the barrel, the slide didn't pull back, and the spent casing failed to eject. The next round didn't cycle. The weapon was now dead until Quint manually cleared the gun.

I still held onto the gun, but it did me little good. Quint was the better one-handed fighter. I'd like to blame the hangover and the earlier falls in the bathroom, but the guy was well-trained. He blocked every punch I attempted and countered them with strikes to my head, neck, and chest. Quint even kneed me, but that attempt hit my outside thigh and not my groin. It was enough to scare me, though, and my grip loosened around the firearm.

Quint jerked the Glock free, and I didn't try to grab it again. Instead, I ran for the back door. I thought Quint might stop and cycle the weapon, but he followed me and clubbed my shoulders with the butt of the gun.

I yanked open the rear door.

The tall man shoved me through the screen door and tumbled after me. We fell down the three steps and landed on the concrete walkway. Chunks of skin tore away from my hands, elbows, and knees. Pain lanced through my groin.

Quint raised the gun over his head like a club.

I yelled "Fire"—the attack command for the German Shepherd sprinting in our direction.

Corporal slammed into Quint and bit his lowered arm. The tall man shrieked and rolled off me, but the dog didn't let go. Quint now clubbed at the dog with the butt of his gun, but Corporal violently shook his head.

I regained my footing and grabbed Quint's free arm.

He hollered, "Get off!"

Using both hands, I twisted the gun from his grip. Then I clubbed him with it. I hit him a second time for insurance. When he went limp, I told the dog, "At ease."

Corporal continued to shake his head and tug on Quint's arm.

"At ease!"

The dog let go and sat next to me. He excitedly panted and watched Quint.

I jerked the slide back on the gun and cleared the spent cartridge.

Then I opened the screen door, and Corporal trotted inside.

***

The cops showed up a few minutes later. It's surprising how fast they respond when you say you're a victim of a home invasion robbery.

Before their arrival, I slipped into a pair of shorts and a t-shirt. My testicles still hurt, and I was worried about a gash on the side of my scrotum. I wiped off the blood that had run down my thigh.

Two patrol units parked several houses away. Three

uniformed officers double-timed toward my home. All crouched as they moved with guns held in the low-ready position.

I opened the door and pushed the screen wide.

The leading officer was a blond woman with alert eyes. She pointed her Glock at me. "Sir, where is the gun?"

"On the kitchen table." I thumbed back toward the house. "It's disassembled."

"Step outside."

I complied with her order and gingerly moved as I went.

"Clear the house," she said to the two male officers with her. Without a word, they moved past her.

"Hold on," I said. "There's a dog in there who won't like it if you just walk in."

The two male officers stopped where they were and waited.

"Let me get him," I said.

The female officer moved so she could peer into the house. "Will he bite?"

"Only if I tell him."

"Don't do that."

"Yes, ma'am." I yelled into the house, "Fall in!"

The dog trotted out and stopped next to me.

"Parade rest," I said it as a single command and not the two-part order I was taught in the academy.

Corporal sat and watched the three cops.

"Go on," I said. "It's clear."

The two male officers hurried by and into the house.

"Is the suspect still out back?" the female officer asked.

"No, ma'am. He vanished after I called nine-one-one."

The officer slipped her gun into its holster and snapped its safety strap. Her silver nametag read *Strong*.

She pointed to the sign on the front door.

"Private detective?" she asked.

"Something like that."

"I think I've heard of you."

After the other officers cleared the house and secured Quint's gun, we went inside. I put Corporal in the backyard and returned to the kitchen where the four of us stood. I wasn't in a hurry to sit.

Officer Strong pulled a notebook and pen from her pocket. "Can you give me a description of the man who broke in and assaulted you?"

She jotted as I spoke. I also told her about the fat man. When I finished, she ripped off the page and gave it to the nearest officer. "Put that in the CAD report, then check the area for anyone matching."

"No problem," the officer said.

"The fat man left in a vehicle," I said. "I heard it leave. I'm not sure how Quint left, but he probably came by car since we had to wait for the other guy to show up."

Strong frowned. "Are you telling us how to do our job, Mr. Cutler?"

"No, ma'am."

She turned to the other officers and nodded. They left and closed the door behind them.

"Mind if I sit?" She pulled out a chair and sat. "Now, let's hear the story again—from the top."

I retold my version of events. She didn't take notes like before. Instead, she studied my face as I spoke. When she didn't understand something, she stopped me for clarification. On those things she immediately grasped, she nodded and muttered words of affirmation. When I finished, she flipped open her notebook.

"So, Suzie?" she said.

"That's right."

"What's her last name?"

"She didn't offer it, and I never thought to ask."

Strong tapped her notepad. "She never mentioned where she lived?"

"No, and I didn't ask that either."

"You guys came back here."

"That's right."

The officer wrote something in her notepad. "How did she get here?"

"She drove herself—a Mitsubishi Eclipse."

"She followed you?"

I nodded.

"Do you remember the license plate number?"

"I don't."

"Was she wearing a wedding ring?"

It seemed an odd question. "No."

"Are you certain?"

"I typically notice them. I noticed yours."

Her thumb rubbed the side of the simple gold band on her third finger. "How do you feel?"

"If you're asking how I physically feel, I'd say I'm fine."

"You don't look it. You should go to the hospital. From what you've described, you want that checked out."

My fingers touched my right cheek, which felt swollen.

"We need some photographs of your injuries." She grabbed her shoulder microphone. After announcing her call sign, she said, "Start a corporal to my location."

The radio squawked before the dispatcher replied, "*Copy*."

She pulled a business card from her notebook and handed it to me.

"Tricia," I said.

"My friends call me Officer Strong."

I raised an eyebrow.

"If you remember anything, that's how you get in touch."

We sat together until a police officer with a camera arrived. He took several photos of my house before focusing on me. The first photo was a full body shot. Then he moved in closer to get my face.

Officer Strong stepped out of the room while he photographed the cut on my scrotum.

Looking down at the injury, it didn't seem as terrible as I first thought. There was already some bruising, but the cut no longer worried me. Maybe it was because I'd seen it a few times, and it no longer bled. Also, the pain had stopped being a sharp stabbing sensation and moved to a dull ache.

"Get that looked at," the corporal said. He packed up his camera and left.

Officer Strong stepped into the kitchen. "All right, Mr. Cutler. I'm leaving now." She pointed to the business card on the table. "If you remember anything, call me. All right?"

"I promise."

"And don't forget to go to the hospital."

***

I brought Corporal inside then double-checked the house locks. Usually, the dog slept in another room because he tended to snore, but I wanted him near today. He slept at the side of my bed. I never even noticed his snoring.

When I awoke, I checked the digital clock on the nightstand. Ten p.m. Nine hours had passed.

My hangover was gone but was replaced by a deep migraine. I rolled over and winced. Carefully, I stood then shuffled into the bathroom. I brought Corporal with me.

After undressing, I realized I probably overestimated my healing ability. My scrotum was black and blue now. It might have been worse than I thought. At least the cut seemed less problematic.

I showered and fought the anxiety of being attacked again. I remembered a story about the *Psycho* actress being afraid to take showers after filming that famous scene where she was attacked. I understood her fear now.

The hot water did little to ease my tension. I took some Ibuprofen.

After I dressed, I went downtown.

***

I found a parking space a block away from O'Doherty's.

The Irish pub's bar sits in a U-shape. That allows a single bartender to service a large group of customers while also providing drinks for the entire establishment. When I settled gingerly onto a stool, the bartender looked up.

"Hey, John."

"Brian."

Concern registered on his face. "You all right?"

"Rough day."

He set a glass under the tap handles and pulled the one labeled *Guinness*. Dark beer flowed. "Want to talk about it?"

"Not really."

Brian glanced around, then leaned in. His voice lowered. "What happened with the blonde from last night?"

"Long story."

"Part of your rough day?"

I nodded.

"Say no more." He stopped the flow of the dark beer but let the glass sit.

"Does she come in here often?"

"Never saw her before."

Brian poured more beer into the glass then handed it to me. "Let me know if you want to order some food." He turned to check on another customer.

Now alone with my thoughts, I tried to disassemble the problem with Suzie.

I replayed our conversation. Not the initial part—that was easy. Instead, the latter part was murky due to a drunken haze. Both Suzie and I were several drinks into our own evenings when we shared a laugh about another patron insisting that she be allowed to show the bar a WSU tattoo on her lower hip. No one cared about her reasoning, but several guys egged her on. The insistent patron lowered her pants then pulled down a portion of her panties to proudly show the ink. That woman ended up with quite a few admirers after that.

Suzie and I were on the opposite side of the bar from where I sat now. Our conversation seemed easy and about a lot of nonsense. When did I realize there was a potential for it to turn into a romantic entanglement? Probably after our third drink together, which would have been my sixth for the night. I think there were one or two beers after that.

I shouldn't have driven home. I'd walked home plenty of times, but she wanted to follow me. She shouldn't have gotten behind the wheel either.

When we finished our clumsy interlude, she left my house. There wasn't an awkward goodbye or a false promise to call the other. She never even asked for my number. It wasn't my finest performance, and I considered her quick exit as proof. All I wanted was sleep.

Did Suzie go home and tell the fat man what we did? Was she that drunk? Was it the alcohol that caused her to be so brazen?

I sipped my beer, but it didn't taste as good as usual.

Suzie knew my last name, but I didn't know hers. We never bothered sharing last names—was that part of her plan? So, how did she know mine? The *John Cutler Investigations* sign on the front door probably gave it away. Heck, maybe she took a business card off my desk as a souvenir.

Did she have a plan that night? Does someone maintain a scheme after that many drinks?

And what led Suzie to go home and tell the fat man about her infidelity? Especially when he had a man like Quint in his employ.

No, she didn't have a plan, I decided. She was drunk and emotional, and she spouted off.

I did that sometimes.

Another sip of beer didn't provide any joy. I pushed it away.

"Problem?" Brian asked.

"Not in the mood." I reached into my pocket and pulled out a ten. I also laid my business card on top of it. "If she comes back, call me."

The bartender nodded. "Will do."

***

I shouldn't have been able to sleep that night because I'd already gotten nine hours earlier. However, I had no problem drifting off again. As before, I double-checked the locks and brought Corporal into the bedroom.

Nightmares pierced my sleep.

In one terrible dream, Quint repeatedly smashed my

testicles with a hammer. When I awoke, Corporal stood next to the bed watching me. His hot breath was in my face.

I pushed him away and went back to sleep even though more nightmares surely awaited.

***

In the morning, Officer Tricia Strong dropped by my house. She knocked on the screen and peered through the open door.

I sat behind my desk, reading the newspaper. "Officer Strong?"

"Can I come in?"

"Yeah, sure."

She pulled open the screen and stepped inside.

As casually as I could, I closed the drawer with my gun in it. I had it open in case Quint decided to return. Corporal stood but remained by my side.

Strong eyed the dog. "I was surprised to see the door opened, but now I know why."

I motioned for her to sit but she declined.

"I'll only be a minute," she said. "Besides, I sit in the car most of the day."

I remembered. I used to be a cop in Seattle. It was only a few years ago that I quit, but it seemed further in the past. A lot had changed in that time.

She asked, "How are you feeling?"

"Better."

"Did you ever go to the hospital?"

"Not yet."

"You're going to be sorry if that turns into something bad."

"They've been hurt before and by much tougher women than Quint."

She didn't smile.

"So, Officer Strong, how do I rate a follow-up from Spokane's Finest?"

"We found a woman in the river this morning."

A pit formed in my stomach. "Suzie?"

"They've fingerprinted the body, and the results should come back later today, maybe tomorrow. But I've got a feeling she's the girl you described. The detectives handling the case asked if you would come identify her."

"I don't know her full name."

"Doesn't matter. It'll link the two cases together."

I folded the paper closed.

***

Strong drove us to Holy Family Hospital. Normally, passengers in a patrol car ride in the back. She made an exception, saying it was due to my injuries. I'd like to think she did it because she trusted me.

Once at the hospital, she escorted me through a maze of hallways until we ended up in a brightly lit room. It was the second time I'd been to the medical examiner's office since living in Spokane.

Officer Strong shook hands with the ME's assistant. She was a short woman with unkempt hair.

"Dora, this is John Cutler. He's here to identify the Jane Doe."

The woman eyed me with medical coolness. She said, "Follow me" and walked through a set of double doors into the next room.

Under a white sheet on the first stainless steel gurney was a body. Dora walked over to the table and pulled a sheet back to reveal the face.

Although the face was bruised and swollen, I recognized her immediately. "That's her."

The assistant covered the body with the sheet again. Officer Strong jerked her head toward the exit, and we left the room.

Once outside, I said, "Not much for small talk?"

"That place gives me the creeps."

***

After Officer Strong returned me home, Corporal and I went into the backyard. While he walked to a corner to do his business, I sat on the steps and thought some more about Suzie.

I replayed the night at the bar. The more I thought about it, the more convinced I became that Suzie was the instigator. I can't remember her exact words, but I'm sure she asked for me to take her home. I know that sooner or later, I would have suggested such a thing, but she did it before I could. So, maybe she did have a plan—find a guy to take her home and then tell the fat man. But for what reason?

And why was Suzie with a guy like the fat man? She seemed to be the type of woman who had her choice of men.

Corporal trotted over and watched me. I petted his head.

Suzie never told me she had a boyfriend or a husband. Even if she had, that likely wouldn't have stopped me. I've slept with married or otherwise involved women before. Unfortunately, not knowing his name left me nowhere to start.

And what about his strongman? Quint was bitten by the dog. Not only should that have hurt, but it probably needed medical attention. Officer Strong said no hospital reported anyone coming in with this type of injury.

Maybe my worrying about things didn't matter. Soon

enough, the cops would discover Suzie's identity via her fingerprints. After that, they would locate family and friends, and they'd continue pulling the thread until they found the fat man.

Corporal and I went inside as the phone rang. I answered it on the third ring.

"Hello?"

There was no answer.

"Hello?" I repeated.

The phone went dead. I stared at the handset for a moment, then hung up. Then I quickly snatched the receiver from the base and dialed *69. The robotic female voice came on and said, *"The number of your last incoming call was 509—"*

I grabbed a pen and jotted the number down on the corner of the newspaper.

Next, I powered up the computer. It hadn't been on in days. My former girlfriend—she used to be my part-time assistant—handled the computer-related duties. She liked those types of tasks. I tolerated them. Once the monitor came alive, I started the internet browser. Then I entered the phone number into the search box.

The computer displayed a bunch of results that didn't make sense. There seemed to be many ads for paid services to help me find a phone number. I scrolled through the first page of results then checked the second. Frustrated, I pressed the power button and turned the stupid thing off.

For a moment, I considered taking Corporal with me. If the recent phone call was to check if I was home, I didn't want the dog left alone. However, leaving him in my truck while I ran errands wasn't the best plan either. And what if something happened to me, and he was stuck in there for an extended time? It might be days before someone found him. I didn't like either option, so I left him in the backyard. It seemed the lesser of two evils.

Climbing into my truck was troublesome. My groin felt tight, and pain flashed when I exerted myself. I headed downtown.

Inside the public library, I headed for the information desk. A woman with frizzy hair turned as I approached. She wore a rather sublime look. "Yes?"

"Where are your Polk directories?"

She pointed to the back of the library. "But we haven't updated them in a couple of years. Why don't you use a reverse look-up on the internet?"

"I tried, but I didn't get the results I wanted."

"Mind if I help?" She walked from behind the counter. I followed her to a bank of computers. "There are some websites that make you pay, but you can always try some of the free ones."

She sat at a computer and moved the mouse. A darkened screen lit up. Her fingers danced across the keyboard and a website popped up. "What phone number are you looking for?"

I pulled the torn corner of the newspaper from my pocket and handed it to her. Quickly, she inputted the phone number and tapped the Enter key. She hovered the mouse over the fourth result—Mackenzie International. Along with the name was an address. "Does this look correct?"

"Might be."

The printer next to the computer buzzed. The librarian grabbed the page and handed it to me. "Isn't the internet great? If you need anything else, let me know." She returned to the information desk.

I stepped into the library's lobby and used my pre-paid cell phone to call Officer Strong's voice mail number. When it beeped, I left a message.

"Officer Strong, this is John Cutler. I might have a

lead on Suzie's boyfriend. I'm going to check it out. It's a business called Mackenzie International. They're located at—" I consulted the printed address and read it off. "Yeah, so, if I find the fat man there, I'll let you know. Or if you get this message, give me a call."

***

The drive to Mackenzie International took fifteen minutes.

During that time, I rationalized why I called Officer Strong. I'd worked with a couple of local detectives before but hadn't kept them in the loop. Was I growing not only as a person but as a private investigator? I'd like to think so.

But there was a part of me that knew the real reason why I called Officer Strong. She was a woman, and I wanted her to like me. It was stupid and immature. That's why I tried to rationalize it away with my growth as a human being.

Mackenzie International was in a dumpy warehouse about five hundred feet from the road. It was hidden behind an aging strip mall that fronted North Market Avenue. That building contained a tack store, a music shop, and a church. I passed the building twice before I realized the warehouse was behind it.

I pulled into the parking lot and put my truck in the spot nearest the exit. When I got out, I tucked my Glock into the back of my jeans.

Mackenzie International's small lobby consisted of four torn leather chairs and a receptionist counter. A silent TV with a rotary dial and rabbit ears stood in the corner. Faux wood paneling lined the walls. It was as if the 1970s stopped by and never left. Behind the desk was a door with a small window that looked into the warehouse.

A young woman sat behind the counter. She wore a black AC/DC t-shirt, and her red hair was tucked behind her ears. Her head was bowed as if she were reading something. She didn't look up from her magazine until I stood directly in front of her. When she finally did, it was with effortless boredom. "Yeah?"

"Is Mr. Mackenzie in?"

She sniffed once. "Who?"

I pointed at the wall and the plywood logo of Mackenzie International. "I want to talk with the guy who owns the company."

"There's no Mackenzie."

"What about Quint?"

The woman squinted. "Nobody wants to see Quint."

"I do."

"What about?"

"A dog bite."

The receptionist lifted slightly from her seat to study me. "Quint's not here."

"Then let me talk with Quint's boss."

The redhead settled into her chair then leaned over to an intercom panel. She pressed a white button. There was a squelch through the building. "Someone is here to see Quint." When she finished, she looked up. "Sit over there."

"I'll stand."

"Suit yourself."

The phone rang, and the receptionist picked it up. "Yeah?" She eyed me. "He says a dog bite." She rose fully from her chair now to check me out. "He seems to be walking fine. Why?" She shrugged. "I don't know. I'll ask." To me, she said, "What's your name?"

"He knows who it is."

The receptionist rolled her eyes. "He says you know

who he is." She inhaled deeply then her brow furrowed. "Yeah, fine. I can do that. Uh-huh."

"Is he going to come out?"

She lifted a finger to quiet me.

"Right. Okay. No, that's no problem. I'll let him know."

I moved closer to the counter in hopes I could hear what was being said over the phone.

From behind me, a male voice said, "Get your hands up."

I glanced back.

Quint was in the lobby. He clutched a revolver and motioned upward with the gun. "Nice and easy."

I faced the counter again and lifted my hands.

The receptionist hung up the phone and returned to her magazine.

"You're good," I said.

She flipped a page. "Quint will see you now."

With a tug, Quint freed the gun from my waistband. "Turn around."

Each of Quint's hands held a gun—his and mine. His left forearm was bandaged.

"Looks like that hurts," I said.

"It did."

"Consider us even."

"Not quite. Walk through the door." He motioned that he wanted me to enter the warehouse.

I eyed the receptionist. "You see what's happening, right?"

She turned another page. "Have a nice day."

"Move it," Quint said.

With a twist of the knob, I opened the door. The hum and spin of electric tools, the hiss of an air-compressor, and a radio tuned to a classic rock station greeted us.

Expensive cars were in various forms of being

stripped. All the high-end brand names were present.

Quint kicked me in the butt, and I stumbled forward. My groin felt on fire again.

"Head into the back room," he said. "The man is waiting."

Several mechanics worked on various cars, but none looked in our direction as Quint and I walked through the warehouse. I thought about running, but I'd never outrun a bullet. Maybe I could jump and hide, but my injury precluded quick movements. In the end, Quint would find me anywhere I hid. He had two guns, and I had none. It wasn't looking good for me.

We walked to a small back office. I opened the door and entered. There were two windows—one back into the warehouse and one for outside.

Seated behind a mahogany desk was the fat man. Expensive-looking paintings hung on light-colored walls. A thick carpet was underfoot. The room was out of place in the dumpy warehouse, but it seemed to fit the fat man like a perfectly sized glove.

"Mr. Cutler," he said. "The gift that keeps on giving."

Quint shoved me forward.

"Please, sit." The fat man motioned toward a chair. "And tell me why you're here."

"You know why."

He leaned back. "You've a rather large ego."

"Among other things."

Quint cuffed my ear, which set off a ringing in my head. I grimaced and held my head.

"Crude, Mr. Cutler. Very crude."

Classic Cutler, I thought. I should learn to make things easier on myself by shutting up. I said, "Is it too late to say I'm sorry?"

"We're beyond that."

I glanced back at Quint. My gun was tucked in his

waistband. He held his gun in his right hand.

"How'd you find us?" the fat man asked.

"You called."

He repeatedly tapped his desk with a single finger. "The call to see if you were home." He shook his head.

"But we hung up right away," Quint said. "There's no way he could have traced it. That takes minutes, doesn't it?"

"Mr. Cutler must have done something with a computer. Is that right?"

I shrugged. "Star sixty-nine."

The fat man eyed his security man. "Technology." He said it like a swear word. "We should have done something right then. I apologize, Quint. You were right." The fat man peered into the warehouse. "This whole thing with the computers and the internet, we're getting left behind. We don't even realize it."

"We got a computer out front," Quint said.

The fat man waved a hand. "That's not enough. Something's going on, and we're not paying attention. If we don't get in on this soon, we're going to be dinosaurs."

"I hear you, but what do you want to do with him?"

The fat man's gaze returned to me.

I sat up straighter.

"We underestimated you, Cutler." The fat man dismissively flicked his hand. "Deal with him.""

Quint kicked my chair. "Get up."

"If he's going to shoot me," I said, "at least, tell me who you are."

"Come now, Cutler, this isn't a movie. Play nice with Quint, and this will go easier for all of us."

Something flashed by the outside window.

"The hell was that?" Quint asked.

The fat man turned to look. "What?"

I leaned to look but didn't see anything.

"Someone ran by." Quint kicked my chair. "Who's with you?"

The fat man struggled to his feet and hurried to the outside window. He pressed his forehead against the glass and looked left then right. "The hell?"

One of the mechanics yanked open the office door. "It's a raid!"

The fat man turned, and his eyes widened. "I can see that."

I stood and looked through the warehouse window.

The mechanic bolted away as uniformed officers fanned out with their guns drawn.

"Stop!" a cop yelled.

Another mechanic shoved open a side door, and daylight flooded the interior. The cop chased after the fleeing employee.

Quint slipped his arm around my neck and yanked me closer to him. The pain in my groin reminded me it was still there.

"What are you doing?" the fat man hissed.

"Getting out of here."

Quint shoved his gun into my back and guided us through the office door. Four cops lifted their firearms. One of them was Officer Strong. All yelled some form of "Drop the gun!"

The tall man jerked me by the neck, and pain lanced through my groin. I dropped like a sack of potatoes. Nothing truly happened, but if he was going to shoot me anyway, I was going to make him do it in front of a bunch of cops.

Quint's arm cinched tighter around my neck. "Stand up!"

I slumped further and put more weight into his arm. This pulled him off balance until he was leaning over me.

"What are you doing?" Quint shouted. He pressed the gun into my side. "I'll shoot you!"

"Drop the gun!" an officer yelled.

"Do it now!" another hollered.

I faked passing out, and Quint struggled to hold me upright.

"You son of a bitch," he said. He let go, and I flopped to the floor. I curled up and groaned.

Quint tossed his gun to the floor then kicked it away. "Don't shoot! I give!"

***

Officer Strong sat with me in the lobby. "Thanks for the heads up, Cutler."

"You're welcome."

Her lips tightened.

"What?"

"That was sarcasm."

"Oh."

"You're lucky I checked my voicemail."

"I had it under control."

She pointed into the warehouse. "He had you by the neck."

"Not at first. That happened after you showed up. Until then, everything was going my way."

Strong rolled her eyes. "What was your plan?"

"It was a work in progress."

"He took your gun away. That was yours in his belt, wasn't it?"

"Am I going to get that back?"

"I'll bring it to you at the hospital."

"The hospital?"

She motioned toward my hands that absently cupped my groin then raised an eyebrow. "Have you been?"

"No, but I'm fine."

***

At Sacred Heart Hospital, Doctor Joel Bohn said, "You should have come in right after this happened."

"So I've been told."

We were in an examination room, and I lay on a table. The hospital gown I wore was pushed above my waist.

"Your cut is bleeding again. This isn't an area to mess around with." He looked up. "I sure as hell wouldn't if this happened to me."

"I'm afraid of doctors."

He leaned closer to check out my scrotum. "You're afraid of me?"

"This is what I consider bad touching."

Bohn frowned. "The bruising and cut both seem superficial."

"They don't feel superficial."

He moved to the nearby cabinet and opened a drawer. "How did that wound happen?"

"I played in the wrong sandbox."

Bohn nodded. "That'll do it. How about I stitch that up, and we get you out of here?"

I raised onto an elbow. "Do we need to?"

***

Officer Strong stopped by while I waited for the local anesthetic to wear off. I felt okay enough to leave, but Doctor Bohn insisted. Strong was no longer in uniform. Instead, she wore blue jeans and a white shirt. Her long hair hung loosely about her shoulders. In her hand, she carried a small paper bag.

"Can you go home yet?" she asked.

"In a couple minutes. They're finishing my paperwork."

"That's good."

I motioned at the paper bag. "Did you bring me something to eat?"

"It might be a little hard to digest." When she set it on the nearby table, it clunked. "But I promised to bring it to you."

"What did you find out about the fat man?"

"Gordon White?"

"That's his name?"

She nodded.

"I think I'm going to keep calling him the fat man."

"You probably figured out what he was into."

"Stolen cars. Chop shop."

"The state patrol's stolen auto unit is still on-site. They've taken over that portion of the investigation. Seems White had orders as far away as Eastern Europe."

"All of this was about cars?"

Strong shrugged. "It's about money. From what the Stolen Auto troopers have put together—and understand this is still preliminary—White had crews stealing cars from Denver and Salt Lake City. They'd funnel them into Spokane. Once they were altered or parted out, the cars were shipped to Seattle. After that, they went to their final destinations."

"Preliminary, huh?"

"It was a pretty good find."

"What about Suzie?"

"Suzanne Welker? What about her?"

I shoved my hands into my pockets. "I don't know. I guess I wanted to know more about her."

"She used to be the receptionist there."

"Really?"

"That's not enough?"

I waggled my elbows. "I want to know more. You know, like why she would go for the fat man."

Strong shrugged. "Who knows why people go for anyone. Maybe she went for him because she saw power. Perhaps she went for him because she saw money. Or maybe, and this is a big maybe, maybe he was nice to her, and she responded to that."

"I don't see that happening."

"Trust me, it happens."

A nurse walked in with a clipboard. "Mr. Cutler, we need you to sign a few things, then you're out of here."

I initialed and signed where she pointed. When I was done, I collected my paper bag. I followed Strong out of the hospital. Once on the sidewalk, she asked, "Are you going to be okay making it home?"

"Would you mind giving me a lift back to my truck?"

"It wouldn't be appropriate."

"Why not? We rode together earlier."

"I was in uniform then, and now I'm not." She lifted her left hand and wiggled the gold wedding band. "I don't ride around with strange men."

"I'm not a stranger."

"You are to my husband unless you want the three of us to go out for dinner."

I raised my hand in surrender. "Never mind. I'll make it home on my own. Thanks for your help, Officer Strong."

"See?" She smiled. "I told you that's what my friends call me. Now, you're getting it."

Echoes of Her

"The cops think she's making it up." Kaylee Springer leaned forward in her chair and put her hands on her exposed knees. She wore a yellow summer dress that stopped mid-thigh. Sandy hair fell to her bare shoulders.

I asked, "How do you know what the cops think?"

"I was there when Mia reported it. I saw it."

Kaylee had just spent several minutes telling me a story about how someone left notes on her friend's car while she was at work. Someone also left unsigned love letters on her friend's car at her apartment and while she was out shopping. When Kaylee revealed where the two women worked, I almost stopped the meeting. The stack of unpaid bills on the corner of my desk bought her a few minutes more.

I shifted in my seat. "All that doesn't say why the cops think Mia's making it up."

Kaylee flopped back into her chair. "What can I say? They didn't believe her. I could feel it."

I crossed my arms over my chest. "Not believing her and thinking she's making it up are two different things."

Kaylee's shoulders slumped. "Great. You don't believe it either."

"I didn't say that."

"Your face did."

I watched the oscillating fan in the corner of the room. "Where did Mia file this report?"

Kaylee cocked her head.

"Did she do it from home or—"

She smirked. "From the club, but that shouldn't make

any difference—."

I held up a hand to stop her. "It shouldn't, I agree."

Kaylee's eyes narrowed. "But it probably did is what you're saying."

"How would you describe the cops who responded?"

She shrugged. "I don't know. My age, I guess. A little younger."

"Early twenties?"

"Them. Not me." She didn't smile when she said it. "Yeah."

"And we keep saying cops, so there were two?"

"That's right."

"Both guys?"

Her smirk returned. "I wouldn't have this problem if there was a woman involved. So, yeah, both guys. Are you starting to see the problem?"

Maybe the officers were distracted by other calls for service. If the friend looked anything like Kaylee, their preoccupation wasn't hard to discern.

"Have the notes increased in their intensity?"

Kaylee's smirk vanished. "They started off pretty harmless, but they've gotten spooky lately."

"Spooky, how?"

"Well, the guy—"

"You're assuming he's a guy."

"Mia doesn't swing the other way."

"That doesn't mean her stalker wouldn't."

Kaylee's brow furrowed. "They would know which way Mia does, so it's a guy. Definitely."

My gaze drifted to the stack of bills on my desk. How badly did I want to pay those?

She leaned forward again. "The notes started with comments about how beautiful Mia was. Don't get me wrong, she's gorgeous, but this guy was saying weird shit. At first, he said things like she was the earth, and he was the moon. Real Romeo and Juliet stuff, but not quite.”

“He wrote poetry?”

“Sort of. Then the letters changed to worshipping her. Really odd. The last couple said she was beautiful while shopping or working out.” Kaylee’s brow knitted. “The guy knows a hell of a lot about her, Mr. Cutler. Where she goes, what she does. You see what I’m saying?”

“Has he ever asked to meet?”

“No, never.”

“And no threats?”

She shook her head.

I rubbed my chin while I thought. The cops were unlikely to do much about it until an overt threat was made. Until then, they’d probably consider it a low level of harassment. “Why didn’t Mia come with you today?”

Kaylee’s gaze softened. “Mia grew up in some Podunk, Oregon town. A couple boys raped her during her junior year.” Her eyes challenged me with that statement. I don’t know what she expected to see, but whatever she found must have satisfied her. Kaylee’s lips pursed, and she inhaled deeply through her nose. “When the cops showed up, they accused her of lying. The boys were the town’s football stars, and their parents were big supporters of the church. It wouldn’t look good to tarnish any of their reputations. You know how it is.”

“Sure.”

“Plus, the boys openly admitted what they had done—with a twist, of course.”

“They said Mia asked for it.”

Kaylee nodded. “They said she had remorse after it was over, and that’s why she called the cops. Most everyone believed the boys. Mia said even her dad believed them. She ran away from home after that.”

I grabbed a pack of cigarettes from my desk. Kaylee

shook her head when offered them. I set them back down without taking one for myself.

"Mia doesn't trust many people, Mr. Cutler, especially the police. When she told the cops about what was occurring, they didn't believe her. She felt like she was back in high school. I'm looking to find out if you'll believe her story before she talks with you. I'm not going to put her into the same situation again."

"How did you find me?"

"I saw your name in the paper."

Had I been paid on time for that job, maybe I wouldn't have to take this one. "Do you know how this works?" I asked. "There are fees and expenses."

Kaylee shrugged. "That won't be a problem."

I knew it wouldn't. I remembered how much money these women made.

"Okay," I said. "I'll talk with her. When does she want to meet?"

"She's working tonight. Can you stop by? She'll make time for you."

A part of me wanted to say no to everything. That I wouldn't meet Mia at her place of employment. That I wouldn't help her find who was sending her disturbing letters. There were too many things with these women that might dredge up something painful from my past. I didn't need that kind of bullshit.

But another part of me desperately wanted to say yes. I wanted to be reminded of why it hurt so bad. I needed to know if the pain was still there.

"Tonight will be fine."

***

That night I drove out to The Red Light District at Stateline, an actual city sitting on the border of

Washington and Idaho. It sat about twenty-five minutes from Spokane. There was a Red Light District in every major city in the northwest. Seattle, Portland, and Spokane all had one. I'm not sure what this small Idaho town did to earn one, but they were among the big boys for strip clubs.

The parking lot was full, and the illuminated sign announced there was no cover on Monday nights.

After I turned off the engine, I sat in my truck for a few moments and listened to the thumping that came from inside the club.

Several years prior, I met a woman named Paige while dispatched to a disorderly patron call at the Seattle Red Light District. We soon found ourselves in a relationship that ended badly. I take responsibility for it. There was something about Paige that brought out the worst in me. Whatever it was, it turned me inside-out and flipped me upside-down.

The fall-out from that time in my life was absolute. I lost my job with the Seattle Police Department, and I lost Paige. Then I moved to Spokane and left my daughter in Seattle with her mother.

I climbed out of the truck and slammed the door harder than necessary.

A muscular bouncer hunched over a security lectern inside the club's small lobby. His lips moved, and his finger trailed along with something he read. He seemed deep in concentration which was no easy feat as the music pumped loudly inside the club.

He glanced up. "ID?"

"Yeah." I reached for my wallet.

"No cover tonight." He waved me in with a flick of the wrist.

A reddish glow bathed the main portion of the club. A DJ stood on an elevated podium in the corner. On the main stage, a thin woman with blond hair clung to a chrome pole. Tables and chairs surrounded three sides of the stage.

Along a back wall sat booths shrouded in darkness. They were for the private dances. In two of the booths, women wriggled intimately on their customers.

A skinny redhead in jeans and a black t-shirt came by. "Something to drink?"

I ordered a Coke and stood near the column closest to the exit.

When the server returned, she studied me. "You okay?"

"Doing great," I lied.

We traded cash for the soda, and she went off to find another customer.

50 Cent's "Candy Shop" played through the speakers hanging from the ceiling. The dancer continued her routine on the stage while I scanned the crowd. A hand settled on my shoulder, and I glanced back. Kaylee Springer stood slightly behind me.

She spoke into my ear. "You made it."

"Wasn't hard to find."

Kaylee pointed at the stage. "Mia's up next. I'll make sure she talks with you after this."

When the music ended, the skinny woman bowed. A table of clean-cut men clapped wildly and cheered.

"Guys from the airbase," Kaylee said into my ear. "Not a big fan."

The dancer waved at the cheering men, then she grabbed her bikini and hurried off the stage.

A stuttering guitar piece pierced the air, and the DJ announced that Mia was up next.

From the back room, a raven-haired woman stepped out and glided toward the stage. She wore a black bra, matching spandex shorts, and platform high heels.

Tattoos covered her white skin. I stared. She was a painted version of Paige.

As if struck by lightning, I stepped back and bumped into Kaylee.

She patted my shoulder. "She's beautiful, huh?"

The intro music ended when Mia took full command of the stage. From the speakers, a low hum growled as she grabbed onto the pole and slowly bent over backward. Her hair touched the floor just before the speakers suddenly pulsed with a heavy metal song. Mia jerked herself upright and whipped around in rhythm with the music. Her eyes were partially closed as she swung her head in small circles.

Kaylee tapped me on the shoulder, and I leaned over so she could yell in my ear. "Rob Zombie."

"Who?"

"The guy singing. He's her favorite."

My attention remained fixed on Mia. The longer I watched her, the less like Paige she seemed. Her body was solid, the kind of thick that comes from working out. It gave her a strange exoticness.

Her long hair fell to the middle of her back. As she moved around, she lifted it up. The center of her upper back was covered with a large tiger tattoo. Asian lettering surrounded the animal. A tribal design ran around her lower back to her belly, making a belt she could never loosen. Another tribal tattoo wrapped her left leg, starting from her knee and ending at her waist. The light reflecting from her nipples showed they were both pierced.

Mia grabbed the pole and swung her body upside down. She pushed herself parallel with the floor and slid slowly down.

As she moved around the stage, her eyes remained slightly closed. Mia seemed oblivious to the crowd.

I glanced at Kaylee. "Is she high?"

"She goes someplace else when she dances."

Mia slowed her gyrations as the song ended. During the brief silence, she opened her eyes and saw Kaylee. Then her eyes shifted to mine.

The next song started, and Mia spun away.

I leaned toward Kaylee. "Tell your friend to come outside when she's done."

She opened her mouth to say something, but I walked off.

***

Sometime later, Mia exited the club with Kaylee by her side.

Mia wore a black Rob Zombie t-shirt, faded Levi's torn at the knees, and a pair of flip-flops. Kaylee wore the yellow dress she had on earlier in the day.

I slipped out of my truck and closed the door.

"Mia," Kaylee said, "This is John Cutler. Mr. Cutler, this is Mia Sandell."

Mia extended her hand. She stood several inches shorter than me. Her eyes were still slightly closed, and she had an almost dreamy appearance. A little steel stud pierced her lower lip, and a small ring looped through her left nostril.

When I shook Mia's hand, I said, "Nice to meet you."

"Kaylee told me about your background. That you used to be a cop."

"A long time ago."

Mia cocked her head. "Is everything all right?"

"You remind me of someone."

"Yeah?"

"A little."

Mia pulled a cigarette from her purse and lit it. "Want

to go somewhere and talk? I've got an hour."

"Where?"

"How about Cruiser's? It's up the way." She pointed in the direction she meant.

I glanced at Kaylee.

"I'll let you two talk," she said. "It's my night off, so I'm going to head home and enjoy it."

Kaylee kissed Mia on the cheek and whispered something to her. When they parted, Mia said, "Should we ride together?"

"I'll meet you there."

She cocked her head again, but this time her brow furrowed. "Whatever." She headed off into another portion of the parking lot.

It was a short drive to Cruisers, but it was enough time to remind myself that Mia wasn't Paige. The two weren't even close. The closest features were hair color and skin tone. That was it.

I was making too much of it. Paige was dead. I didn't kill her, and I couldn't have saved her. She kept secrets and told too many lies for me to do that. So, why did I want Mia to be anything more than what she was?

The reason was simple. Because I felt guilty for all things Paige. It was absurd and juvenile.

I turned into the parking lot of Cruisers and climbed out of my truck. A red Mazda RX-8 pulled into the stall next to me. When Mia slipped out of the car, she said, "Ready?"

Inside Cruisers, we grabbed a table near the stage. Since it was Monday night, no band was scheduled to play. A server brought us a couple of light beers, and Mia ordered some fries.

Mia said, "Kaylee's great, isn't she?"

"She's worried about you."

"We've been friends for a while. Almost like sisters."

Her eyes were fully opened now that she was away from The Red Light District.

"So, you have questions," she said.

"I do. Mia's your real name."

"That's not a question."

"Why don't you use a different name for the stage?"

Mia shrugged. "I should, but—" She stood and turned around. With one hand, she lifted her t-shirt while the other hand pulled down the waistband of her jeans. In the middle of her tattoo belt was her name.

"Huh."

When she sat, she said, "If I call myself Trixie or something else, everyone will know it's a lie. I can't break the fantasy, or they won't pay."

"The fantasy."

She leaned in and studied me. "You know the fantasy?"

"All men know it."

"Not like you, huh?" Mia's eyes narrowed. "You know it intimately."

I stared at her.

"Someone hurt you with it."

"Not so bad," I lied and looked away.

"Was she a dancer?"

When I didn't respond, she asked, "What was her name?"

I looked down at the cement floor.

"Please tell me."

My eyes returned to Mia. She seemed genuinely interested. "Paige," I said.

"And that was her real name?"

"It was."

"I remind you of her?"

"I was wrong." I lifted my beer for a sip but hesitated.

"Do you still want to help?"

I shrugged.

She wasn't Paige, and I needed the money.

"In that case—" Mia reached into her purse. "—you probably want to see these." She set a small stack of letters on the table.

For several minutes, I perused them. As Kaylee had mentioned, the earlier ones contained some clumsy poetry—if I was anyone to judge. That kind of writing lasted for a few letters before it switched to simple adulation. Had the handwriting been different, I would have argued they came from other people.

The tone of the letters shifted when the handwriting did. Those of awkward verse were of wonder. Angst seemed to be the undercurrent of the most recent.

But nowhere in any of the letters was there a clear threat to harm Mia. Years ago, some might have considered this type of thing the behavior of unrequited love. I saw it differently—a creeper working his way up the scale.

I slid the letters back to her. "You have no idea who is leaving these for you?"

"No."

"They don't sound like an ex-boyfriend?"

She smiled. "Uh, no. None of mine would ever try the poetry stuff."

"Have you had any problems at the club?"

"Nothing more than usual, and nothing that would lead me to think it's from a guy who would write this type of thing." She tapped the top letter.

"Where do you live? What city?"

"Liberty Lake."

"That's a pretty expensive area."

"I do okay."

I thought about Kaylee's story about Podunk, Oregon. "What brought you up here?"

"I worked a club in Portland. Unfortunately, I had a jealous boyfriend who liked to beat on me when he got drunk."

"Your work must have made him bitter."

She picked up a cold French fry and examined it. "When I finally smartened up, I broke it off and moved."

"Why didn't you call the police?"

Mia dropped the fry. "Because he was a cop."

I started to say something and stopped.

She said what I was already thinking. "We seem to have some parallels in our lives, John."

I didn't respond.

"Did you ever hit Paige?"

"Never," I said. "I would have died for her."

And I meant it.

***

We met the next day—Tuesday—to further our discussion. Not much should have changed since the night before, but the break allowed me some time to think about her problem. We met in the afternoon at a Borders Bookstore in Spokane Valley, a midpoint between where we both lived.

I got there early and waited by sitting on my truck's tailgate. When Mia arrived, she parked next to me. She sipped from a Jitters and Shakes coffee cup as she approached.

She motioned toward the cigarette in my hand. "Got another?"

"Last one." I extended it to her.

She took it and inhaled.

"What're you drinking?" I asked.

"A tall skinny with sugar-free vanilla." She inhaled once more on the cigarette and handed it back. "With a kiss of cinnamon."

"Sounds complicated."

"It's good."

"I'll bet," I said unenthusiastically. "Anything new happen today?"

"Just a normal, boring day. Woke up. Went to the gym. Then came here."

I flicked ash from the cigarette. "No problems at the gym?"

"Didn't even get looked at once."

"I find that hard to believe."

She shrugged. "It's a woman's gym. There's a reason I go there. What about you? Have you learned anything?"

"It hasn't even been a day."

She raised an eyebrow. "What have you been doing?"

"Nothing."

"Doesn't seem like I'm getting my money's worth."

I shrugged. "I get paid for results. Not for how busy I look."

She playfully patted my knee. "Maybe the client wants to see you busy."

"Yeah," I said and slipped off the tailgate. "Then you've got the wrong guy."

"Geez, lighten up."

I closed the tailgate.

Her face was serious now. "Have you decided on a course of action?"

"There aren't a lot of things for me to do yet. I can check on past boyfriends if you want."

"None of them would act like this."

"Which leaves one option."

"The club?"

I shrugged.

"You want to come watch the crowd?"

"Not really."

"But you'll do it?"

"If that's the job."

Her face relaxed, and a smile slowly spread across her lips. "You'll be my bodyguard like that guy from the movie. What's his name?"

"I'm not a bodyguard, and it could get expensive to have me standing around studying the crowd."

"Maybe I think it'll be worth it."

"Why not have one of the bouncers do it? Tell them what to look for."

Mia shook her head. "They've got other things to worry about. I want you focused on me."

"We'll do it for a few nights. See how it goes."

She toasted me with her cup. "If you say so."

"When do you work next?"

"Thursday night. My days off are Tuesday and Wednesday. The weekends are the real moneymakers, but we all have to work a couple slow days."

I walked to the driver's door and climbed into my truck. "So, I'll see you Thursday night."

"Kevin Costner."

"Huh?"

"That's the guy from the movie. You know, the one with Whitney Houston and that song everybody liked. C'mon. You had to have seen it."

"Thursday," I said.

She watched me drive away.

***

When I returned home, I took my dog for a walk. We headed downtown to see what was going on in the city.

Corporal was a German Shepherd with a snarl that makes people step back. His previous owner was a retired Marine Drill Instructor who taught him to obey Drill and

Ceremony commands.

When the dog and I arrived at Riverfront Park, I said, "Halt." I found a dry patch of grass and sat. Then I told Corporal, "At ease."

The dog lay next to me and watched the commotion in the park. Kids and parents were everywhere. I liked the park when it was quieter. I'm hesitant to let the dog off his leash with a mass of people around. I'm not worried about what he would do. He's trained. Rather, I'm afraid of what some freak might do. The dog is my best friend.

"You should see her," I said.

The dog panted as he watched a group of college-aged guys throwing a Frisbee.

"She sort of looks like Paige."

The dog yawned, and his gaze followed an older man who jogged slowly by.

"You never met her, but she's still in my head." I tapped my temple. "I can't get her out. Do you know what that's like? When a girl gets in your nose? Twists you all up until you feel like you're going to suffocate?"

Corporal rolled over and closed his eyes.

"You seem unimpressed."

We hung out in the park for thirty minutes then returned home. I turned Corporal loose in the backyard before checking the blinking light on my answering machine.

"Hi, John, it's Mia. Is this really an answering machine? Hello, two-thousand-late, it's time to dump your landline. Yeah, so, anyway. One of the girls sprained her ankle, so I'm going to cover her shift tonight. I'll start at nine and will go through until two. I'd appreciate it if you could come by like we talked about."

The answering machine beeped.

***

I returned to The Red Light District around a quarter till nine and lingered in my truck. I didn't want to be there. Too many memories of Paige strangled the moment.

When an RX-8 pulled into the parking lot, I slid out of my truck. Mia climbed from her car and held another coffee cup from Jitters and Shakes.

"Thanks for being here," she said.

I shrugged. "It's the job."

She smiled. "This is the first time I've ever paid anyone to watch me dance."

"I'm not watching you. I'm watching the crowd."

Her face flattened. "Paying for results. I got it."

Mia led the way into the club and headed toward the dressing room without looking back. I ordered a coffee from the gal behind the bar. With a Styrofoam cup in hand, I found a spot in the corner that afforded the best view of the floor and the private booths.

For a Tuesday night, it was busier than I expected. Half the club was full of customers from every demographic. Some men seemed wealthier than the others, and they got more attention from the dancers stalking the floor. A couple watched from near the stage. Perhaps they were married and fulfilling some kink—to each their own.

Four dancers worked the night, and each of them had a three-song rotation.

Chastity was an early twenties black woman with pretty eyes and a slight overbite. However, her figure drew attention away from that imperfection. She danced to popular hip-hop songs and spent her off-stage time in a private booth with a heavyset white guy in his sixties.

London was roughly my age and had the bored gaze of

someone who'd worked the stage too long. When it was her turn, she half-heartedly danced around the pole. For whatever reason, though, she had a collection of admirers who wanted her time in the private booths. She didn't perk up over there either. Maybe those guys enjoyed the worn-out look in a woman's eyes.

Then there was Chyna with a Y—that's how the DJ introduced her. She wasn't Asian, and she wasn't exotic. What she was, however, was enthusiastic. Somewhere in Chyna's background must have been time with a cheerleading squad. She broke out several moves during her routine reminiscent of a high school pep rally.

After Chyna left the stage, Mia strolled out to the same stuttering guitar intro as before. She wore a black sports bra and black Volleyball shorts. There was no reason to watch her perform—I was there to work. Besides, I didn't need to create any similarities between her and Paige.

When the first song in her set kicked in—an obnoxious heavy metal tune—some guys in the crowd jumped with excitement. Stateline was in northern Idaho, after all. Several customers flashed her the devil's horns while she slinked about the stage. She gave them double horns back which wound them up further.

She noticed me watching and winked.

Frustrated at being caught, I turned away.

Two more heavy metal songs finished her rotation. One of them I knew—"Highway to Hell." When she finished her set, Mia collected her clothes and left the stage. A couple of minutes later, she returned from the back room. She was in her clothes again although I couldn't forget how she looked on the stage.

Almost immediately, she was approached by a young, white male in his early twenties. He smiled awkwardly and said something to her. Mia nodded and slipped her hand into his. She led him to a booth as Chastity returned to the stage.

Mia danced for the kid for one song before they broke apart, and he paid her. I'd like to say I watched her to make sure she was safe, but I knew why I did. I sipped my coffee and pretended it didn't bother me.

She walked over and bumped her shoulder into mine. "See anything you like?"

"No one stands out."

"Yeah? I saw you looking."

"Momentarily distracted."

"Right." She walked off in search of another customer. There were more around who wanted her attention.

Five hours passed that way. The women rotated throughout the night. When they weren't on stage, they worked the booths. It was easy to ignore the other women. When Mia danced, I found myself drawn to her. While she performed private dances, I struggled to keep my attention on the crowd.

When the night ended, I waited until the last customer was out the door, then I exited. The bouncers locked the doors behind me.

I leaned against my truck and waited.

Fifteen minutes later, Mia walked out. "Feel like getting something to eat?"

"I'm tired."

"Yeah, okay." She briefly glanced away. "So you know, I'm working tomorrow night, too."

"I thought it was your day off."

"Scarlett's ankle is pretty bad. I told her I'd cover her shift again. So, you'll be here?"

***

The next night passed much the same way—five hours

of ignoring Mia while observing the guys in the crowd. The other women never impacted me—not even Kaylee, who danced under the stage name of Skye. I didn't notice any of them.

Yet Mia continued to affect me, and it had nothing to do with her nakedness. It seemed to be worse when she was clothed. Emotionally, I mixed up the past and the present. I don't know why my feelings were jumbled. Maybe I never fully resolved the Paige stuff. Hell, there was no 'maybe' about it. I had stuffed those feelings back down until I thought they crumbled into nothingness.

Perhaps this was God's way of screwing with me— like he cared that I existed.

Mia stopped by throughout the night to make small talk. On one of her visits, several of the guys in the crowd turned in our direction. I lifted my chin toward the looky-loos. "If one of those guys is your stalker, they're going to know I'm your bodyguard."

"Fine with me."

"I'm your scarecrow now?"

"There are worse jobs in the world."

I eyed her.

"Plumbers, for example. They'd be happy to trade jobs with you." She pointed at Kaylee, who was up on stage. "Getting paid to watch her."

"I'm not watching—"

"Yeah, yeah." She faced me again. "What are you doing after?"

"When the club closes? Going home."

"Let's get something to eat."

"Everything will be closed."

She shrugged. "Come over to my place then. I'll cook us some eggs. There's beer in the fridge."

"I need some sleep."

Mia frowned and thumbed toward the stage. "Listen, I

don't normally—" She never finished her thought. Instead, she walked away.

I watched the thinning crowd as the night ended. When the bouncers finally escorted us out, I stayed by my truck until Mia appeared.

"Will you be here tomorrow? My normal rotation starts again."

"This is going to get costly for you."

"I haven't had any problems since you showed up."

"You weren't having problems every night, were you?"

"Still."

I said, "I can't do this forever."

"Why not?" Her eyes bored into mine.

I broke the gaze and climbed into my truck. She stopped the door from closing.

"So, tomorrow night?"

"I'll be here," I said.

There was a flash of victory in her smile. It was the same grin Paige gave whenever she got her way.

***

I headed back to Spokane but didn't go home. Instead, I went to a friend's house. When Stacy Mathers opened the door, she was bleary-eyed and in a long t-shirt.

"John?" she whispered. Her voice was raspy from sleep. "The hell? What time is it?"

"It's late."

She shushed me then leaned back to check something on a nearby wall. "It's two-thirty. Are you drunk?"

"Not an ounce."

"A call would have been nice."

"I should go."

"Like hell." She rubbed her eyes and stepped out of

the way. "Just be quiet. The kids are asleep."

She closed the door behind me. "Let me brush my teeth, okay?"

A while back, I saw Stacy's sister intermittently. Stacy disapproved of that whole set-up because of how her sister treated me. Her sister was divorced and back on the dating scene, but I was well below her social stratosphere. We'd met at the club where I worked, and I turned out to be an easy call for her whenever the mood arose. Stacy found the whole thing despicable. I ended things when I wanted to build a relationship with a nice girl—that relationship didn't last.

When Stacy's marriage fell apart, she called me. Only to talk, she said. She wanted a man's perspective on what went wrong. It was an odd request from a woman I'd never met. She sounded hurt and lost. Our first meeting ended with a drunken encounter in my truck. Since then, we'd become convenient lovers much like her sister and I once were.

When we finished, Stacy lay her head on my chest. "Is everything okay?"

I turned to her in the darkness. "Yeah, why?"

"You were rough."

"I'm sorry."

"Don't be." She patted my chest. "It was different, but let's not make a habit of it."

I fell asleep for a couple of hours but snuck out before either she or the kids woke up.

***

On Thursday night, two more girls I'd never seen before were in the rotation with Mia and Kaylee. There were now six in all. They rotated throughout the night, sharing stage time and working the booths when they could. The crowd behaved, and I kept my gaze away from Mia whenever she was on stage.

It was almost midnight when a mid-thirties white male walked in. His blond hair was short and combed to the side. He wore black slacks, a blue polo shirt, and dress shoes. He moved through the club like a panther—on the hunt and ready for a fight.

Mia was in the back getting ready. She was up next.

Eminem's "Shake That" boomed through the club while Chastity danced on stage. Panther briefly watched her, then curled his lip. He soon found a chair and dropped heavily into it.

Kaylee approached Panther, but he waved her off. She said something with a smile, but he didn't reply. Instead, he continued to scan the room. When his gaze landed on me, he stopped. Panther squinted, then cocked his head in a questioning manner. If I had to guess, he was sizing me up.

The song ended and several in the crowd politely clapped for Chastity. Panther, however, continued to study me. Chastity grabbed her clothes from the stage and hurried to the back.

When the stuttering guitar intro started for Mia's entrance, Panther's attention snapped to the stage. He sat upright as if on an important job interview. His hands opened and closed into fists several times.

A new hard rock song started, and Mia pranced around the stage. Panther's shoulders bounced in time with the rhythm, and he sang along. The only words I could understand were "Crazy Bitch."

Panther scooted to the edge of his seat and bounced intensely with the song. He lifted his arms above his head and swayed. He seemed to be in a world of his own.

On stage, Mia had yet to remove either her top or bottoms.

The first song ended and immediately transitioned into a new one. There was never dead air space. It was another hard rock song that I hadn't heard before. I was thankful for that.

Mia removed her top, and Panther fell back into his chair. He laughed and covered his face with both hands. It was like he was having a moment solely with her.

I walked over to the bouncer and motioned to Panther. "He been in before?"

The bouncer nodded. "Every Thursday night. Like clockwork."

"Got a name?"

"Nah. You worried about him?"

"Has he ever caused trouble?"

The bouncer shook his head. "Not once."

"Looks like he's hooked on Mia."

"No shit. And she's paying you for this?"

Mia's last song started, and she wriggled out of her black shorts. Panther rotated his neck then rubbed his face. He shook his head and laughed loudly. The bouncer might not have seen a problem with the guy, but he gave me the heebie-jeebies.

Panther wriggled in his chair almost as much as Mia did on stage. When the song ended, Mia grabbed her clothing and hurried backstage. Panther rested in his chair. He looked spent as if he might have just sprinted a mile. His chest rose and fell heavily with each breath.

A minute later, Kaylee was on stage, and Panther ignored her. He leaned forward and put his hands on his knees. His head was down, and he muttered to himself.

When Chastity walked by, I gently grabbed her by the arm. The girls knew me by now, and she didn't flinch at my behavior. "Do me a favor," I said, "tell Mia to see me when she comes out."

Chastity studied my face. She must have sensed the

urgency in my request because she headed immediately to the back.

When Mia finally reappeared, Panther perked up and motioned toward her. She acknowledged him but held up a single finger to tell him to wait. Then she headed toward me.

"What's up?" she asked.

"The guy in the blue polo shirt."

Mia glanced over her shoulder then waved at Panther. When she faced me again, her smile was soft. "That's Kern. You've got nothing to worry about. He's a regular."

"Your stalker is probably a regular. Know his last name?"

"We're not those types of friends."

I looked over her shoulder. Kern glared at me.

Mia's hip jutted to the side. "Is Kern the guy or not?"

"I don't know, but he's the only one that has made me take notice so far."

"Well, if he's not, I'm going over there."

"Don't dance for him."

Mia's lips twisted. "He's been around a lot longer than those letters. It's not him. Trust me."

She spun and headed toward Kern. He stood as she approached but kept his eyes on me. Mia thumbed back in my direction as if she were trying to explain something. Kern angrily shook his head and looked at the floor. She gently touched his face, which caused him to nod. Then she took his hand and led him to a back booth.

I knew what would happen now. I didn't need to watch it. I'd seen it before with Paige, and it tore me up. Of course, I was in love with her. I wasn't in love with Mia, and I didn't need to confuse myself with pretending to be.

If she wanted to dance with Kern, then so be it. She

was a grown woman, and she could make her own decisions. Besides, she said she knew him longer than the letters had been coming.

I walked over to the bar and got a cup of coffee. There was no reason to watch the crowd now. No one acted weird beyond Kern, and I knew where he was. When he left the club, I would walk outside and get the license plate number off his car. Then I'd call in a favor from a cop friend. Maybe he could tell me Kern's last name and if he had any criminal history.

Until then, I would stand here, drink my coffee, and feign to be okay with it.

A woman screamed, and I glanced over to the booths.

Kern pushed Mia to the floor, and his hands were around her throat. She slapped and clawed at him to get free.

I ran across the room and tackled him. He hadn't seen me coming, and his head collided with the base of the booths. He was rendered unconscious, but that didn't stop me from winding up to punch him in the face. The bouncer caught me by the crook of the arm and yanked me away.

"He's out," the bouncer said. "Stand back."

I reached down to Mia and helped her to her feet. She allowed me to shield her as the bouncer dragged Kern from the club.

The music never stopped, and Kaylee remained on stage. She stood naked and watched us. A couple of guys loudly groaned their complaints. Mia looked toward her friend and waved. Kaylee slowly returned to dancing, and the crowd's grumbling stopped.

I escorted Mia into the back room, where she sat in front of a mirrored desk.

"You okay?" I asked.

She nodded.

"What happened?"

"Kern was mad."

"What for?"

"I told him you were my bodyguard, but he didn't believe me. He said you were my boyfriend. He called me ungrateful."

I pulled over a chair and sat next to her. "We probably didn't think that through—how some of these guys might react to me being here."

"I thought about it," she said. "Trust me, I did. I figured I'd lose some tips, maybe some dances, but never anything like this."

"The cops are going to come. They'll want a statement."

She nodded. "I'll give them one—fuck Kern."

"So, maybe it was him after all."

"Yeah," she whispered. "After the cops get what they want, I'm calling it a night."

"Probably a good idea."

***

"This is a bad idea."

Mia led me into her bedroom. "I know what I'm doing."

I let her convince me to drive her home from the club. First, she told me that she was still emotional after the attack. Then she said she didn't want to go into her apartment alone. She didn't seem scared, but I wanted to believe it and not for chivalrous reasons.

After entering her apartment, I knocked over a baseball bat she kept next to the front door. I started to pick it up, but she said, "Leave it."

Now, she stood at the foot of her bed.

"I should go." I didn't make a move toward the door.

"I want you to stay." She pressed her body into mine and looked up into my eyes. "Help me feel safe."

"This will affect our professional relationship."

Her arms wrapped around my neck and pulled me down to her.

I said, "I won't be able to think clearly around you any longer."

"That's a bad thing?" She closed her eyes and pressed her mouth against mine.

I pulled back. "Please, Paige, don't—"

Mia opened her eyes.

"Shit."

She shook her head. "I'll be whoever you want."

***

In the morning, she clung tightly to me. I got up and showered. After dressing, I went to the kitchen and rifled through her cabinets.

"What are you looking for?"

I glanced over my shoulder. Mia leaned against the counter. She wore only a black Slipknot t-shirt.

"Where's your coffee maker?" I asked.

"I don't own one. Go to the place across the street and get us both a cup. I'll grab a shower and be ready when you come back."

I pulled her to me, but she turned her cheek.

"Not now," she said. "I stink." She told me her coffee order.

"You drink that every day?"

"Don't make fun. Order it, and if you forget, tell them it's for me. They'll probably remember."

When she moved for the bathroom, I headed for the door.

Across the street was Jitters and Shakes. It sat on the end of a small retail strip center. A line of cars circled the building to get to the drive-through window. I'm sure the other tenants in the building were thrilled with the amount of waiting vehicles clogging the parking lot.

Inside the business, the aroma of coffee hung thick in the air. I stood in line behind a couple of college-aged girls as they ordered their drinks. Both texted on their cell phones while they ordered.

When they were done, I stepped to the counter. The barista turned to me and smiled. He had shaggy blond hair and a pooka-shell necklace. His nametag read *Austin*. "What can I get ya, boss?"

"Black coffee and a tall, skinny, sugar-free vanilla latte."

He tapped on the register. "Cup a joe and a tall, skinny, sugar-free. Got ya. Anything else?"

"Oh, yeah. Put some cinnamon on top."

Austin nodded. "Cinnamon."

"Just a kiss."

"A kiss?"

"That's what she said. Not me."

The barista's hand hovered over the register. "This for Mia?"

"How'd you know?"

Austin tapped a button then announced a total. "You guys friends or something?"

"Or something." I handed him several bills.

He slipped the cash into the register and handed me my change. "Didn't know she had a boyfriend."

"You know her well?"

"We talk every morning." He made eye contact now. "Except this one."

Austin turned to make the coffees. I watched him, but he never glanced back. When he finished, he put two cups on the counter.

"You ever send her letters?"

His brow wrinkled. "Excuse me?"

"Maybe leave them on her car?"

Austin leaned forward. "What's your problem, man?"

I picked up the coffees. "No problem."

"Seems like you have one."

"Only asking questions."

Austin crossed his arms. "Ask them somewhere else."

***

I walked into Mia's apartment and found her on the couch. Her hair was wet, and she now wore a Soundgarden t-shirt and ripped blue jeans. A magazine was spread across her lap, and a cigarette dangled between two fingers.

"Delivery service," she said. "I can get used to this."

I sat next to her, and she tossed the magazine onto the floor.

"What should we do this morning?" she asked.

"How often do you go to that coffee joint?"

"Every day. Why?"

"What do you know about Austin?"

She smirked. "What about him?"

"He likes you."

Mia rolled her eyes. "It's a crush."

"No kidding."

Her brow furrowed. "How'd you pick up on that?"

"He noticed your order."

"That means he pays attention to his customers."

"Has he ever asked you out?"

She shrugged a single shoulder. "Once. Made a real

mess of it. I let him down easy that he wasn't my type."

"Does he know what you do?"

She waved a hand. "I doubt it. He's never asked, and I've never told him."

"You only know him from the coffee shop?"

"He waves to me when he's on his balcony, and I'm on mine."

"He lives here?"

"Yeah," Mia said and got up. She pointed out her window to the building on the opposite side of the parking lot. "He lives over there. He's the apartment with the bicycle on the balcony."

Third floor, second apartment over.

"Do me a favor and wait here. I'll be right back."

"Where are you going?"

I left Mia in her apartment and trotted over to Austin's place. I took the stairs two at a time and was almost out of breath when I got to his apartment. I knocked on the door and waited. It was a simple precaution to make sure he didn't have a roommate.

In the corner of the landing was a plant. A simple doormat lay in front of his door.

Would I break-in? I was leaning toward it. I'd committed a burglary before to solve a case. Checking out Austin might lead to nothing, but it would make me feel better.

When no one responded to my knock, I tried the doorknob. It was locked. I glanced around to make sure no one was looking.

Should I break-in? Was it worth risking a felony? All the guy did was ask me about Mia. But he said she was there daily, and he lived directly across the complex from her. That wasn't a lot to go on, but it was more than I had since I started working with Mia.

I prepared to kick the door in. The potted plant in the

corner caught my eye and I hesitated.

They say discretion is the better part of valor.

I reached into the pot and felt around. Nothing. Next, I flipped up the doormat and was rewarded for taking an extra minute—a single key. I picked it up and slipped it into the apartment's lock. The door opened, and I stepped inside.

I wished I had thought to have brought my gun beforehand, but it was still in my truck's glovebox.

The apartment was tidy, and I moved quickly through it. The bedroom was no different. On the dresser was a photo album. I flipped it open to reveal several pictures of Mia standing on her balcony. She seemed unaware that she was being photographed.

Pictures of Mia filled the entire book. All seemed to be taken without her knowledge. She lay by a pool—the apartment community was in the background. Carrying the photo album, I moved to the nearest window. There was a view of the pool from there.

In other pictures, Mia walked across the apartment community's grounds.

However, there were photographs of Mia entering and exiting her gym. Entering and exiting a grocery store. There were even a few of her entering The Red Light District.

There weren't any of her exiting.

I closed the photo album and put it back where I'd found it.

***

Inside the coffee house, an espresso machine hissed. A female barista smiled as I approached the counter.

"Is Austin here?" I stood on my tiptoes to see into the backroom. It didn't help.

"He said he wasn't feeling well, so he went home."

"How long ago was this?"

She shrugged. "I dunno. Twenty minutes or so."

Austin hadn't gone home. I was just there.

I ran across the street and into the community's parking lot. Then I sprinted up the stairs, taking them two at a time. Mia lived on the third floor. I twisted the knob when I got there, but it wouldn't open. When I left, it was unlocked.

Loudly knocking, I said, "Mia, let me in."

No response.

A second knocking didn't bring anyone to the door.

I stepped quickly back before kicking the door. It didn't budge. I kicked it again—this time near the handle. The door popped open. I moved into the apartment, grabbed the baseball bat from the floor, and held it over my shoulder like Sammy Sosa.

"Mia?" I called.

Austin was in the kitchen, hurriedly pulling open drawers.

"Where is she?" I asked.

He spun around and lifted a large knife. "You!"

I gripped the baseball bat tighter.

Austin stepped closer. "Why couldn't you leave well enough alone?"

"I called the police!" Mia shouted from the bedroom.

"Time to go, Austin."

His eyes narrowed as he moved toward me.

"Drop the knife," I said.

"No."

He hunched his shoulders and lowered his height like an animal preparing to spring. When Austin leaped, I swung for the fences.

***

Mia stayed locked in her bedroom, and I remained standing over Austin until the cops arrived. After checking Austin's vitals, they immediately called for medics. For a moment, I thought I had killed him. He hit the floor as if dropped from a plane. He never moved after that.

The bedroom door opened, and Mia poked her head out. "Is it safe?"

I waved her out, and we moved to the corner of the living room. The first officer on the scene approached us. His nametag read *Olsen*. "Are you the one who called, ma'am?"

She nodded.

"What happened?"

"Austin showed up and wanted to confront John. When I told him he wasn't here, he freaked out."

Olsen thumbed toward the body on the living room floor. "Is he a former boyfriend?"

"He works at the coffee shop." She pointed in the direction of the business. "I see him like five times a week, but he's always been sweet."

"And you didn't invite him over?"

Her face pinched. "No. Never."

The cop eyed the now stirring Austin. "What provoked him?"

"I've been getting these letters and flowers on my car. I didn't know who they were from."

"And you think they're from him?"

"We do," I said.

Olsen's gaze shifted to me. "And you are?"

"John Cutler," I said. "Private investigator."

"Why does she need a private investigator?"

"Because a couple of your guys were called out previously and decided it wasn't real enough to take seriously."

Olsen's face flattened. "So, you decided to handle the situation like Mark McGwire?"

"When he came at me with a knife, all bets were off."

"He had a knife?" Olsen turned to survey the floor. He found it near the couch. "Let me secure that, and we'll continue this discussion."

***

"So, it's done," Mia said.

We stood outside in the parking lot. The ambulance had taken Austin away, and the cops were leaving the scene.

"For real this time," I said.

She glanced around. "It feels weird."

"What does?"

"It was Austin. He always seemed so nice. Why would he leave me those letters?"

"He was weird. Who knows why they do what they do?"

"Yeah." She headed for her apartment but stopped when I didn't follow. "Aren't you coming up?"

"I need to go home. Feed the dog. That type of thing."

She smiled. "You have a dog?"

"A big one."

"I have to work tonight," she said.

"I know."

"Are you going to come by?"

I shook my head.

"Because of last night?"

I nodded.

"I'll call in sick."

"Don't do that."

She walked back to me but didn't reach out. "Are you

brushing me off?”

“I wouldn’t do that.”

Mia crossed her arms. “You don’t want to spend time with me?”

“Of course I do, but I can’t change who I am, and I’m not going to ask you to change who you are.”

She touched my face. “What I do would eat you up.” It wasn’t a question.

“The moment I allowed myself to care, it would kill me.”

“And you would care? You know that?”

I pulled my keys from my pocket. “I’ve got to go.”

When I yanked the door to my truck open, she said, “Don’t forget to send me your bill.”

“I won’t forget.”

I didn’t check the rearview mirror as I left the parking lot.

Sister Wives

The woman stared like she expected I would know what she wanted.

She stood in the doorway with a mirror-perfected pose—a hip jutting to the side with a manicured hand resting on it. A ponytail of long blond hair fell far past her shoulders. If she was over thirty, it was only by a year.

"Well?" she said through deep red lips. "What do you have to say for yourself?"

I stood so I could see over her shoulder. Outside, a bright-red Mustang convertible sat in front of my home-office. The sun glinted off it, but no one waited for her. My gaze shifted back to the woman as I returned to my seat.

She stood almost six feet tall in sandals. Her white shorts highlighted tanned legs, and the spaghetti-strapped blouse barely contained her.

"Miss, I have no idea what you're talking about."

"It's missus." She crossed her arms. "You should know that. You've been following me."

My chair dropped into a reclined position. "I've been following you?"

"That's what I said."

"You're sure it's me?"

"Damn right, I'm sure."

I brought my chair forward. There were several cases currently underway, which meant watching multiple people. This woman wasn't one of them. She'd be hard to forget.

"My husband sent you a check," she said. "I saw it."

"You saw the check?"

"Yes. Well, the cleared check with the bank's stamp showing it had been paid and processed."

I cocked my head.

"You are John Cutler, aren't you?" She pointed around the room. "And this is your office?"

"That's what the sign on the door says."

She frowned. "Don't get cute. If my husband paid a detective a thousand dollars, I want to know why?"

"Who's your husband?"

Her eyes flashed around my office. "It doesn't look like you have a lot of people paying you a thousand dollars."

"Lady, if you don't want to answer my question, I can't help you."

The woman pursed her lips. "Martin Glass."

"Huh."

"Care to fill me in now, Mr. Cutler?"

Martin Glass had given me a check for one thousand dollars which I happily cashed two weeks ago. I followed Martin's wife and took photographs of her with a local real estate agent. The pictures were basic photos of them holding hands and walking into the boyfriend's house. Martin wanted more than that, but they were the best photos I could get without breaking into the home and standing in the bedroom.

The woman studied me and waited.

I met her deep blue eyes and calmly said, "I'll look into this."

She slapped her hip. "But you said, huh. Why did you say that?"

I shrugged.

Her eyes narrowed as blossoms of cherry arrived on her cheeks. "Why did he hire you? What does he think

I'm doing?"

"Who are you?"

Her lips pursed together. "You know."

"Lady, on my life, I've never seen you before."

She crossed her arms again.

"Trust me. I would remember someone like you."

A couple of moments passed before she said, "Brandy Ryan."

"Not Glass?"

"Martin insisted I retain my name. He wanted me to have my own identity. He's sort of a feminist that way." Suspicion flooded her eyes. "You've honestly never seen me before?"

I raised a hand as if I were standing before a bailiff. "Hand to God."

Brandy's distrust faded.

"Where did you see this cleared check?" I asked.

She started to step into the house but stopped. "May I come in? It seems like something I should ask now."

I motioned toward a chair in front of the desk.

When Brandy moved, the screen door closed automatically and latched. She sat and crossed one smooth leg over the other. Her nose scrunched. "You really shouldn't smoke in here. It makes your house smell."

"I've quit, but the smell lingers. About that check?"

"I saw it on the internet."

I didn't know that was possible.

"You get it on the bank's website." Brandy must have noticed my confusion because she added. "You click it, and it comes up."

I lifted the nearby telephone and said, "I call to check my balance."

"It's 2007. Get with the times. You have a computer."

I glanced at the silent monitor on the corner of my

desk. My former girlfriend previously handled all things related to the computer. I wasn't incapable, merely reluctant.

My focus returned to Brandy. "This account you checked—it's a joint one?"

Her face flushed.

"Does he know you have access?"

"If he did, he would change the password." Brandy shifted in her seat. "It's not like I do anything bad on there, Mr. Cutler. I only want to know how much Martin has. That's all. He's sort of secretive about some things."

"And money is one of them?"

She nodded. "He was brought up poor, so he has some triggers when it comes to it."

"But you check his accounts anyway?"

Her features hardened. "I'm not proud of it. Call me insecure if you must."

I leaned on the armrest of my chair. "We all have our issues."

Brandy looked around before continuing. "When I saw he had written a thousand-dollar check, I wanted to know what it was for."

"Why not ask him?"

"I can't do that."

I tapped the armrest. "Because he'd know you were snooping into his accounts."

She lowered her chin. "Would you like your woman combing through your finances?"

"If I had a woman, I don't think I'd mind." I said it with unnecessary flirtatiousness and regretted it immediately. However, Brandy didn't seem to notice. At her age, she'd probably grown immune to that tone.

"Well, Martin would mind. Besides, it's obvious why someone hires a private investigator. If my husband thought I was cheating on him, he'd lie about it if confronted."

"Why would he do that?"

"To make me feel safe. Martin's afraid of confronting me, so I came to you for the real story."

I thought back to the man I met. "He's afraid of confrontation?"

"I didn't say that. I said he was afraid of confronting me. There's a difference."

I pulled my chair forward so I could rest both arms on the desk. "Are you happily married?"

"Are you a private investigator or a marriage counselor?"

"You avoided the question."

"Am I happily married? Yes, I am." After a moment, she added, "I think so. Now with this, I don't know."

"Have you ever cheated?"

She crinkled her nose. "No. Never." This she said emphatically. "I love Martin. I would never do that to him."

I leaned back in my chair and set my hands back on the armrests. "Would you like me to ask Martin why he wrote me that check?"

Brandy blinked several times before saying, "You said he didn't."

"I'm as confused as you are, and I'd like to know what's going on."

She thought for a moment. "Will doing this thing cost me?"

"No."

"Thank you." She grabbed a pen from my desk and wrote her name, address, and cell number on the back of one of my business cards. "In case you need to get in touch with me."

Her phone number had a 208-area code, and her address was in Coeur d'Alene.

I set the card down. "Is Martin home?"

"He's in Indianapolis doing some consulting."

"When do you expect him home?"

She shrugged. "I don't know. That's how his jobs are. Could be tomorrow. It could be next week, for all I know. It seems like he travels every week. I usually don't pressure him, but if you want—"

"That's all right. Let me do some checking before we pressure."

"I'd appreciate that."

Brandy stood and extended her hand. I reached over the desk and shook it. Her skin was cool to the touch.

She said, "Thank you for looking into it."

***

After Brandy left, I pulled a thin manila folder from a nearby filing cabinet. It was labeled in pencil—*Martin Glass*. There weren't any photographs of his wife or her lover. Retaining pictures of infidelity didn't seem like a big deal at the time. However, I now saw the value in maintaining a copy.

My handwritten notes were limited:

Alicia Glass, 32, brunette

Involved with Roger Gribble, a real estate agent for Inland Realty

Gribble lives at 2723 W. Rockingham Drive

Need photos of their relationship

Three weeks ago, Martin Glass came to my office. He feared his wife was cheating on him. If I could prove Alicia was doing such a thing, then Martin wanted a divorce. The photographs would be used in the proceedings since Martin worried about paying spousal maintenance—Alicia was unemployed. She stopped working after they married.

I explained my rates, but Martin Glass was a dealmaker. He wanted extra motivation behind my effort. He offered an initial rate of one thousand dollars if I could get the pictures within twenty-four hours. Every day after that, the rate would drop by $100. I told him that at some point, the money wouldn't be worth it.

He said, "Don't let it get to that point."

I agreed and figured I could call off the job if the pictures didn't pan out in a couple of days.

Alicia Glass was careless with her extracurricular activities, and I got the photographs her husband wanted. Unfortunately, they were tame—Alicia holding the hand of a man I suspected to be Roger Gribble as they entered the Glass home.

I tried to remember what Gribble looked like that day. Probably early forties. Tanned and fit. And his hair seemed a little shaggy, but it seemed a lot of guys wore it that way now. Maybe he followed the trends.

Martin wasn't happy that those were the best pictures I could get. We met back at my office.

"That's Gribble, right?"

He looked up. "Yeah. Gribble. That's right." He seemed distracted. It must have been the pictures of his wife that agitated him. Martin returned his attention to them. "I could have taken these."

"But you didn't."

"I could have." Martin nodded. "They'll have to do."

"For your court case?"

Again, he looked up and appeared momentarily confused. "Right. That's right."

"I can take more if you want."

Martin shook his head. "This will be fine, but if I need you in court to testify…?"

I hoped it wouldn't get that far. I hated going to court. "I'll be there. Additional fees will apply, of course." I sounded like a late-night television commercial.

"Sure, sure." He reached into his suit jacket and removed a filled-out check—one thousand dollars. The payee line was blank. "I didn't know if you wanted it made out personally or to your business. Doesn't matter to me."

And now, here I was rereading my notes and trying to remember what went on then.

Martin had said his wife's name was Alicia, not Brandy. They lived in Spokane, not Coeur d'Alene. Alicia was a brunette, not a blonde.

So now, new questions arose. Who was Brandy Ryan, and why did she think Martin Glass was her husband?

I called Martin from my office phone. It rang several times then went to voice mail. I left a message. "This is John Cutler. Give me a call. I'd like to talk with you about that job I did."

A few moments later, my cell phone buzzed once—a text message. The job has been paid. Please, don't contact me again.

I texted Martin. Call me.

It took a few minutes, but the phone rang. When I answered, Martin said, "What do you want?" His voice was hushed but hurried. There was noise in the background.

"We need to talk."

"There's nothing to talk about. You've been paid."

"Yeah, but—"

He said, "You're not getting anymore."

"I'm not trying—"

He hung up.

I called him again, but this time it went directly to voicemail.

Now, I was at a crossroads. I could ignore the whole thing and let it go away. Maybe the tall blonde wouldn't come back. Perhaps she'd get the answers to her questions from elsewhere. But then, I would never know what had really happened, and that didn't sit well with me.

If Martin Glass was already married to Brandy, then why did he have me follow Alicia and her lover. Who the hell were they to him?

I stared at the notes in the file and tried to figure out a game plan. If Martin didn't want to answer my questions, there were two others who might—Alicia Glass and Roger Gribble. I was taught 'ladies first,' but I ignored that rule and grabbed the phone book from the lower drawer in my desk.

As I searched the white pages for the I section, I thought about looking up a scanned copy of a check on the internet. How the hell would something like that work? My fingers paused in their search. Maybe I should use a computer to look up this phone number. No, I decided, the phone book was still quicker. After finding the number, I placed a call.

"Inland Realty," a woman answered.

"Roger Gribble, please."

"A moment."

The line clicked, and a man cheerfully said, "Hey, this is Roger. How can I help?"

"Mr. Gribble," I said, "my name is John Cutler. I'd like to ask you a couple of questions."

There was silence on the other end of the phone.

"Mr. Gribble?"

"I'm sorry, I've gotta go. I'm very busy right now." He hung up the phone.

Two men had hung up on me in a manner of minutes.

What the hell was going on?

Damn it, I thought and tossed the phone book back into the lower drawer. I grudgingly pulled the keyboard to me and powered on the computer. Then I opened the internet browser and typed in 'Martin Glass Spokane.'

Not much came up on the man. There were a couple of articles referencing his name and a boundary line dispute, but that was about it. The search engine tried to convince me I was looking for a glass repair company on Martin Street.

Brandy Ryan's search results were a treasure trove of sports-related articles. She was a high school volleyball star who went on to play at Arizona State. After her graduation from college, though, it seemed like she had disappeared from the world.

Next, I typed in Alicia Glass Spokane. It found an employee named Alicia at one of the glass companies on Martin Street, but that was the best search result for the local area.

Finally, I typed in Roger Gribble. There were plenty of photographs of the real estate agent. As soon as I saw his photograph, though, I knew I had a problem.

Roger Gribble was Martin Glass. Or rather, Roger Gribble was pretending to be Martin Glass.

Had I slowed down at the beginning of this case, maybe I would have avoided this incident. All I needed to do was what I was doing now. What did it take? Ten minutes of keyboard clicking?

But Martin—correct that, Roger—baited me into sloppiness by offering me a thousand dollars. That was more money than my daily rate warranted, and I should have been wary of it.

If something's too good to be true—I didn't finish the thought.

***

After six, I headed up to Roger Gribble's house on

Rockingham Lane. I could have gone out to the Glass home in Coeur d'Alene, but Brandy lived there, and she already told me Martin was out of town. There was no reason to see her yet.

The house was on the South Hill and overlooked the Qualchan valley. A manicured front lawn surrounded the brown brick home, and flowers lined the sidewalks.

The doorbell rang in a pleasant *bing-bong* manner. A minute later, a woman with brunette hair opened the front door. "Yes?"

Alicia Glass wore black yoga pants and a white t-shirt. A light sheen of sweat covered her forehead. Dressed in workout clothes, the curves of her body were far more noticeable now than through the lens of my camera. She was several inches shorter and several years older than Brandy.

"Hi," I said. It was the simplest way to start this conversation.

"Hello." She rested her hand on the door jamb. "Can I help you?"

"This might be a funny question, but whose house is this?"

Alicia's brow furrowed. "For real?"

I nodded.

"It's mine."

"And your husband's?"

"*Mine.* My parents gifted it to me. Are you looking to buy? There are plenty of other homes on the market." Alicia pointed down the street. "There are two over there. The owners of the yellow one need to get out quick so you might be able to get a deal."

I pulled a business card from my back pocket. When I handed it to her, she studied it.

"Private investigator?"

"Yes, ma'am. John Cutler." I stuck out my hand. "And

you are?"

"Alicia Murphy." She didn't accept my hand. "What's this about?"

"Have you ever heard of Martin Glass?"

"He's my husband. Why?"

I pointed inside the house. "And he lives here?"

Alicia's face flattened. "You're not looking to buy this house, are you?"

"Do you know Roger Gribble?"

She glanced around the neighborhood. Her voice lowered. "What do you want?"

"Is Martin out of town?"

Alicia stepped back and partly closed the door. "I don't know what's going on here, but I don't like it."

"Ma'am—"

"Go!"

She closed the door and spun the deadbolt.

***

The following morning, I headed to the county courthouse and requested the records on the Rockingham Lane home. While I did it, I wondered if someday this might be done online, too—much like the cleared check thing that Brandy had told me about.

Several minutes after I turned in my request, a county clerk returned with the information. The house was currently owned by Alicia Murphy. The home was gifted into her name seven years ago, and it was recently assessed at $267,000.

Martin/Roger lied and said Roger Gribble owned the home. Had I taken this simple step, too, I could have proven as much. But did I ever do this with any of my other cases? No. I took my clients at their word, and so far, it hadn't bitten me.

Why would Martin/Roger lie about that?

And who was the man in the pictures with Alicia?

As angry as I was at Martin/Roger, I was angrier with myself. The job seemed to be a slam-dunk, and the easy money blinded me.

***

I waited until Roger Gribble left the offices of Inland Realty shortly before noon. Perhaps I should have cornered him at his work, but that location seemed too much in his favor. Some of this job is playing hunches. And since I was already behind in the game, I needed to think strategically now.

He drove downtown and stopped into Niko's for lunch. Roger hunkered over the wooden bar and scowled into his glass. It seemed a little early for a drink.

Roger Gribble stood over six feet tall and looked like an aging linebacker. He wasn't fat, just a little soft around the middle. His hair and beard were cut neatly. He wore a dark blue suit with a modern cut. His crisp white shirt was unbuttoned at the collar, and his red tie was loosened.

When I sat on the elevated chair next to him, Roger's eyes shifted to me.

"Martin," I said, deliberately using the name he gave me.

He leaned away to get a better view. "You."

"You don't look happy to see me."

"I told you over the phone that our business was finished. Whatever you're doing now, leave it alone."

"I can't do that."

A server with dark red hair brought a plate of mixed greens and put it on the bar. "Can I get you anything else?"

"No, this will be good. Thanks." Roger eyed me. "Why can't you do that, Cutler? Why can't you leave it alone?"

"Because you're not Martin. You're Roger."

He slowly put his drink on the bar and faced me. "You're mistaken."

"No," I said. "You're Roger Gribble."

He shifted his weight and put one foot on the floor.

"But I looked Martin up on the internet."

"Yeah. What did you learn?"

"Not much."

Roger smiled. "So, there you go."

"But I'm figuring things out."

His smile faded. "Yeah? What's that?"

"That he's married to two women, but I'm guessing you already know that. What I don't under—"

Roger shoved me, and my elevated chair tipped backward. I crashed to the floor and hit my head against a nearby potted plant. When I recovered my footing, several people surrounded me and expressed their concern for my safety.

Unfortunately, none of them managed to slow Roger Gribble's exit. He had slipped out the door. There weren't many places a guy like him could run. I could find him easily enough.

But that left me with a nagging question.

Why did Gribble want photos of Alicia and the other man entering her own home?

***

She showed up at my house around eight p.m. and knocked on my door.

My German Shepherd barked immediately. Corporal's prone to do that.

I ordered, "At ease," and the dog went silent. He followed me to the front door. I pointed to the rear of the house and snapped my fingers. His previous owner hadn't taught him that, but the dog knew what I wanted. Corporal trotted away.

After I opened the door, Brandy stepped inside.

I asked, "What are you doing here?"

"Your message said it was urgent."

"You could have called."

Brandy jutted her hip to the side. "You said it was urgent. I figured meeting in person was better, so I drove over."

"From Coeur d'Alene?"

"What's the big deal?"

I motioned her toward a chair, and I sat behind the desk. We resumed the positions we had taken on her first visit.

"Well?" she said. "Are you going to tell me what's so important?"

"Is Martin still on the road?"

Brandy nodded. "Indianapolis."

"How long has it been?"

"A couple of weeks."

"What's he do?"

"He owns a consulting firm. Something with factories to help them be more efficient. Blah blah. I don't get the whole thing."

"But you've talked with him since he's been gone?"

Brandy shrugged. "Not really, no. But he's texted. Mostly little things like 'I miss you' and whatnot. That's what he does when he gets busy. He'll call when he can. He often goes out to dinner with clients and has drinks. They're in a different time zone—three hours sooner than we are."

"So, the texting isn't weird?"

Her face pinched. "It's gone on longer than normal, but is it weird? I don't know. I don't like it, I'll tell you that much, but Martin can be finicky. He has his quirks, and I have mine. We deal with them."

"Have you heard of a guy named Roger Gribble?"

Brandy smirked. "Now, I know you're investigating me."

"I promise I'm not."

Her eyes searched mine. "Roger is my ex-husband."

"Excuse me?"

"I didn't think that needed further explanation. I was married to Roger. Now, I'm married to Martin."

"Was he a decent guy?"

"Roger was a jerk. That's why I left him."

I shifted in my chair. "Were you having an affair with Martin?"

She blanched. "What kind of question is that?"

"I'm trying to understand what's going on. It's not meant to be rude."

Brandy frowned. "I'm not that type of girl, Mr. Cutler. Roger and I weren't compatible. He was needy, and I wasn't. When I told him that I wanted out of the marriage, he didn't take it well. He accused me of cheating which I didn't. I swear."

"Do you talk with Roger now?"

She rolled her eyes. "Why would I? Oh, he calls sometimes and leaves me messages. You know, trying to convince me to take him back, but I never will. It's been almost two years. Move on, I say. Besides, I love Martin too much."

"Describe Martin for me."

"You've met him."

I frustratedly waved. "Imagine I didn't."

"He's forty-two and looks great. Goes to the gym every day. Has a trainer. Tans a couple times week. He wears his hair longer than most men, but I like it. I think that's why he does it. And he's a little shorter than me." She shrugged. "But I'm okay with it. A lot of men are shorter than me."

I closed my eyes and remembered the day I took photos of Alicia Murphy and her lover—the man supposed to be Roger Gribble. The way Brandy described her husband sounded very much like the man I photographed Alicia Murphy with.

When I opened my eyes, I said, "Let's take a ride."

She crossed her arms and set her jaw. "I'm not that kind of girl."

"That's not what this is about."

***

When we arrived at Alicia Murphy's house, it was nearly ten o'clock. No cars were in the driveway. There weren't any windows in the garage, so checking for vehicles wasn't an option.

I knocked on the front door until heavy footsteps hurried about.

Roger Gribble yanked open the door. He was still in the suit he wore earlier. In his right hand, he clutched an aluminum softball bat. "Get out of here."

"Is Alicia home?"

He pointed the bat at me and waggled the end. "I mean it."

"When did you find out about Martin and Alicia?"

Gribble pushed the bat forward until it touched my chest. "I'm warning you."

"Roger?" From behind me, Brandy's voice sounded uncertain.

I stepped to the side so Gribble could see her standing at the bottom of the stairs.

"Brandy?" he said.

She moved up one stair. The confusion on her face was easy to read. "What are you doing here?"

Gribble lowered the baseball bat. "I can explain."

From inside the house, Alicia Murphy asked, "Roger, who is it?"

He glanced over his shoulder. "I've got this."

Alicia came into view now and looked out at us. "Who is that woman, Roger?" Her gaze shifted to me. "You."

"I'll take care of him," Gribble said.

"I don't know what he's been telling you," I said, "but whatever it is, he's lying."

Gribble shoved the tip of the bat toward me. "Leave."

I asked Alicia, "When's the last time you heard from Martin?"

Gribble faced her. "Don't answer that."

Brandy moved up another step. "Why are you asking her about Martin?"

Alicia stepped forward. She kept her eyes on Brandy. "To answer your question, Mr. Cutler, Martin is out of town, and he texted me today. And to answer yours, Martin is my husband. What's it to you?"

Brandy glared at the brunette. "Martin is *my* husband."

Alicia waggled a finger. "You're confused. Martin doesn't go for tramps."

"I'm not the one cheating on my husband."

An evolutionary signal must have occurred between the two women because they screamed in unison. Alicia rushed by Roger as Brandy hurried up the stairs. The two women met on the small porch and then pirouetted back down to the lawn, where they collapsed into an ugly heap of beauty.

The aluminum bat swung past my head and clanged against the house. Gribble shoved a shoulder into me and knocked me off the porch. I stumbled for several steps as

I struggled to maintain my balance.

The baseball bat arced down as if Roger was chopping wood. I jumped, fell to the ground, and rolled onto the sidewalk. Roger advanced with the bat over his head. He brought it down, and it loudly clanged against the concrete.

I hurried to my feet and hunched, prepared to tackle the man on his next swing.

"Roger!" Brandy and Alicia hollered together.

Gribble paused long enough to look at the women. He made a mistake by taking his eyes off me, and I took advantage of it. I crashed into him like a blitzing linebacker hits a rookie quarterback. Roger landed on his back, and the bat skittered away.

He covered his face and prepared to be punched. Without a weapon, though, Roger Gribble was no threat. I stood and stepped away. Roger rolled onto his stomach to see the two women standing together. Both watched him with wild eyes.

***

Roger Gribble sat in a recliner and flexed his jaw. He looked for an escape route, but there wasn't one.

Alicia perched on the couch across from him. Brandy stood next to me. I clutched the aluminum bat in my right hand and rested it across my shoulder—a batter waiting for his chance to swing.

"Alicia," I said.

"Huh?" She turned her attention to me. I kept mine on Roger.

"How long have you been married to Martin?"

"Three years."

Brandy tsked and looked away.

"And Alicia," I said.

"Yeah?"

"When did you first meet Roger Gribble?"

Alicia's gaze landed on the realtor. "About a month and a half ago when I was at the gym."

"Did he tell you he knew Martin?"

"No."

"Did you know Brandy used to be married to Roger?"

Her eyes narrowed further. "He never told me."

"Brandy divorced him a couple of years ago then married Martin."

Alicia looked at me. "Wait. When did this happen?"

"About a year ago," I said.

"But Martin is my husband."

Brandy shrugged. "You seem to have something else going on."

Alicia stood abruptly.

"Hey!" I said, "relax." Both women looked at me, and I pointed the bat at Roger. "Let's stay focused on what's important here."

Alicia resettled onto the couch.

To Roger, I said, "I bet you were surprised when you discovered Martin had two wives."

His face flushed. "Screw you. Call the cops. I didn't do anything wrong."

"Maybe we don't want the cops involved," I said. "Maybe we want to have some old-fashioned justice." I slapped the bat into my open palm.

Roger's eyes widened, and he looked at both women. "You wouldn't let him."

"Better start talking," Brandy said.

"Yeah," Alicia agreed.

Roger shook his head. "C'mon. This is Martin's fault. He married you both. Not me. The guy even made them legal, too. One marriage certificate in Washington. The other in Idaho." Roger fought back a smile.

"Congratulations. You're sister wives."

Alicia and Brandy eyed each other.

Roger sneered at me. "You're supposed to be a professional. You think you would've figured that out, but you didn't."

"I figured you out."

"Barely." Roger started to stand, but I put both hands on the bat's handle and lowered my stance. He dropped back into his chair.

I asked, "What did you do when you found out?"

He petulantly crossed his arms. "Call the cops. You're not going to hit me."

I looked at both women. "We've got a choice. Martin's missing, and I think Roger knows where he is. Either we call the cops to deal with Roger, or you step outside and let me jumpstart the truth by smacking him around."

"Hold on!" Roger exclaimed.

Alicia stood. "I'll wait outside."

Brandy's lip curled. "I'm good staying."

Roger abruptly stood. "Wait a minute!"

My hands tightened around the handle in preparation to swing.

The realtor raised his arms in surrender. "Now, wait a damn minute! I'll talk."

"Get started," I said.

He flopped back into his chair. "Finding out Martin was married to them pissed me off. Why should he get them both? I mean, he's not anything special."

"Yes, he is," Brandy said.

Alicia eyed her.

"I'm sorry, but he is."

Alicia slowly returned to the couch.

Roger inhaled deeply before continuing. "Anyway, I called him on it."

"What did you say?" I asked.

"That I was going to rat him out. After I paid him back, of course."

"Paid him back for what?"

"He took Brandy away."

Brandy threw her arms in the air. "Damn it, Roger. He didn't take me away from you. I left you, then I found him. How many times do I have to tell you that?"

He shook his head. "I don't see it that way."

Before Brandy could respond, Alicia spoke. "I was payback?"

Roger's eyes landed on Alicia.

She lowered her head. "Son of a bitch."

Brandy pointed. "See? This is why I left you."

I pointed the bat at Roger. "Keep talking."

He rubbed the side of his face. "I kept calling Martin and telling him I was getting closer to Alicia."

"Oh, God," she muttered.

"Every night, I called and gave him a status report. What could he do? Nothing. Because if he tried, I would expose him to both Brandy and Alicia. He had to take it."

The two women eyed each other again.

"Sometimes," Roger said, "I told him I called Alicia at work or took her to lunch. When she and I finally hooked up, you should have heard him. It was beautiful—the tears and the threats. I wish I could have recorded it."

Brandy sat next to Alicia and held her hand.

Roger smirked. "The whole thing drove the guy insane, but he couldn't do anything. He was boxed in. I had him. His whole world was built on lies." Roger eyed the women. "And you sit there, thinking he's a good guy. He played you both."

Alicia's head remained lowered. She whispered, "I didn't do anything that he wasn't already doing."

Roger scooted to the edge of his chair. "That's right,

Allie, you didn't."

Brandy held Alicia's hand with both of hers and softly talked with her.

"Listen," I said to bring Roger's attention back to me. "Why did you pose as Martin and hire me?"

"Because I needed the proof to show Brandy."

The tall blonde looked up, but something in this revelation caught the other woman's attention, too.

Alicia's face darkened. "You didn't do that to get even with Martin." Her lip quivered and her voice rose. "You did it to get her back!" She jumped to her feet and stepped across the room. She slapped Roger, but he bent to avoid the strike, and she hit him alongside the head. This seemed to frustrate her, and she slapped his arm several more times. "You bastard!"

When Alicia finally stepped back, Roger looked to Brandy. "I still love you."

Brandy shook her head. "No. Never. Not a chance."

Alicia slapped Roger once more, this time across the face. She returned to the couch and sat. She turned into Brandy and hugged the other woman.

"I still don't understand the posing," I said. "You could have taken the pictures yourself."

Roger stared at me but didn't respond.

"Unless you wanted to create a history of something. Like Martin spying on Alicia maybe? Would that be an alibi somehow? I'm not seeing it."

The real estate agent looked away.

"Answer me this. How did you get a check from Martin to pay me?"

Roger looked at his hands but remained silent.

I tapped his knee with the baseball bat. "I'll have them step outside."

His head jerked up. "All right, relax, will ya? I told Martin to give me a thousand-dollar check with no name written on it. I thought it would be funny—no, ironic is the better word. I thought it would be ironic if I used his own money to pay for the pictures that would ruin his life."

"But the cleared check led us all to this moment."

Roger tilted his head. "Someone found it?"

Brandy looked away from Alicia, who still cried into her shoulder. "I found it. I thought Martin was spying on me, that he didn't trust me. You caused all this hurt. It's what you do. That's another reason why I left you."

"I'm sorry."

"Sorry's not going to cut it. Where's my husband?"

Alicia lifted her head from Brandy's shoulder and faced Roger. "Do you know something about Martin?"

His eyes flicked away.

That's when I knew the truth.

***

The police found Martin Glass buried in the woods near Ione—about an hour and forty minutes north of Spokane. The body was discovered on a large piece of forest acreage recently sold by Roger. Since no immediate development was planned, Roger figured it was a good place to stash a body.

Roger told the cops that Martin Glass attacked him and that he defended himself. He claimed he never meant to kill his rival. Roger stated that Martin simply fell and hit his head on the corner of a marble coffee table.

Martin Glass never woke up from the blow.

Roger hid the body because he knew that the death would look suspicious.

He was right.

***

The day after Roger Gribble was convicted of murder, a red Mustang pulled to a stop in front of my office. My door was open, and I sat behind the desk. When Brandy Ryan stepped out of the car, she turned and noticed me watching. She waved and headed up the sidewalk.

Now, she stood inside my office. She wore a pair of Levi's, brown sandals, and a man's long-sleeve shirt. I wondered if the shirt had belonged to Martin.

"I wanted to come by and say thank you for what you did."

I stood and walked around the desk. "I'm sorry that it ended badly."

Brandy shrugged. "Martin married Alicia first. He was never really mine. That's taken some getting used to."

Another car pulled to the curb. A door opened and closed, and Alicia Murphy soon appeared on the sidewalk. She wore a pair of white pants and a turquoise blouse. A pair of oversized sunglasses sat perched on top of her head, tucking her hair behind her ears.

I glanced at Brandy.

She smiled. "We're taking a trip together. She's actually pretty nice."

"Are you two…?"

"Don't be ridiculous. Martin made us sister wives. It's time we got to know each other."

Alicia opened the front door. "Hi, John."

"Alicia."

"Did she tell you we're taking a trip?"

"She didn't tell me where but yeah."

"Jamaica. I've never been."

"Me neither," I said.

"Want to go?" As if realizing her implication, Alicia crossed her hands like calling a runner out at home. "Strictly platonic."

Brandy nodded. "No funny business, but you should come."

"I appreciate the offer," I said, "but I'll pass."

I shook hands with both women, and we said the little things people do when it's likely they won't see each other again in this life.

They left then and got into their respective cars. I imagined them heading toward the airport, catching a flight to the Caribbean, and laying in their swimsuits on some sandy beach.

Hell, maybe I should have gone. For the next hour, I tried to convince myself that I could be platonic friends with a couple of beautiful women.

Eventually, I gave up that lie and took the dog for a walk.

Remo Lightly

I looked up from the newspaper when I heard the knocking at the front door. I'd been in the middle of an article about the robbery of Every Day is Pay Day, a short-term loan business on North Hamilton Street, when the insistent tapping started. I closed the paper and stood.

"Hold on," I hollered.

My office is in the living room of a two-bedroom bungalow in Spokane's West Central neighborhood. Maybe I should have put the office in the front bedroom, but it seemed more professional to have people step into an office rather than a living room.

I opened the door to find a guy in his late forties. He had longish salt and pepper hair, a droopy mustache, and deep wrinkles around his eyes. The guy wore a Jimi Hendrix t-shirt, faded blue jeans, and dirty gray running shoes. He held the screen door open and looked expectantly at me. "John Cutler?"

There was a sign on the door that said as much, but some folks need the reassurance that a simple "Yeah" brings.

"Can I come in?"

I stepped back. The screen door shut behind him. When he flicked his hair away from his shoulders, the tell-tale scent of marijuana and patchouli oil wafted through the room.

"Hey, man, I'm really glad I found you." He thrust out his hand. "Remo. Remo Lightly." He grimaced. "But just one Remo. Remo Lightly. But the way I keep saying it, makes it sound like two, but it's just one."

"I get it. Remo."

"And before you ask, no, I wasn't named after the old

book series."

My brow furrowed. "What series?"

He pointed at a chair. "Can I sit?" He sat without waiting for me to answer. "That's mostly anyone ever thinks about when they hear my name. Well, not you, but most folks."

I stared at him. The guy had sort of a disarming quality to him.

Remo continued. "My mother was Italian, and she had a brother, Uncle Remo. He wasn't her uncle. He was mine, but you probably figured that out."

"Yeah, I got that."

He chuckled. "Shit, I'm nervous. Anyway, I'm named after him." He paused, then added, "Without the uncle part, but you probably figured that part out, too."

"I did."

"See?" Remo snapped his fingers. "That's why you're a detective. You're smart."

I sat in the chair behind the desk. "You came here with a problem, Remo?"

"Right. Yeah. Definitely."

"What's the issue?"

He leaned forward and looked about as if searching for someone else in the room. "Have you ever been to confession?"

"Like at church? No."

"Me neither, but you get the point."

"You want to confess a sin, Remo?"

He pulled back and laughed. "Heck no, not me." He rolled his eyes. "But I guess I sort of have to, I mean, so you'll help me."

"Tell me what's going on."

"But if I confess my sins to a preacher, he can't—"

"Priest."

"Huh?"

I said, "Confession is with a priest," but I probably should have let Remo roll with his question and kept the correction to myself.

"Yeah. Right. A priest. The dudes with the stiff white collars. Anyway, if you confess to them, they gotta keep it a secret. Like take it to their graves and shit."

"I think that's the rule."

"What about you?"

"I'm not Catholic."

He laughed again. "C'mon, man. If I tell you something, do you keep it to yourself? Like we're in confession?"

I shrugged. "Depends. If you tell me that you murdered someone, then no, I don't have to keep that to myself. I'll probably tell the cops right away."

"I haven't murdered anyone."

"In that case, tell me what you did, and we'll see if we can work together."

"Okay, okay. So where should I begin?"

"Probably at the beginning."

He waved me off. "That's too far back. Here's the thing—I worked a heist."

That's the actual word he used—*heist*. It jumped out because no one ever uses it in polite conversation.

"What did you steal?"

"Me, personally? I didn't steal anything. I was the lookout. Every heist needs at least one of them. I think. Maybe not. I haven't been a part of many. Actually, this was my first."

I inhaled and held my breath. This already sounded like a wild goose chase. Unfortunately, I didn't have anything to work on that morning, and Remo Lightly did hold a strange sort of charm. I could afford to spend a few moments listening to a story. "Why don't you start at the beginning."

He sighed. "That's probably the best. I'm not doing so good starting in the middle. So, yeah. I've got this friend, Charlie. You don't need his last name, do you? Wait. Did I tell you my last name?"

"Lightly," I said, "and I thought you were Italian."

"No, man. That was my mother. Lightly is English." He lifted his finger. "Chip-chip-cheerio, my good man, and all that jazz. My father's people come from Lancashire or some shit. At least, that's what my grandfather always said."

I stared at him.

"But you don't care about the Lightly ancestors. What were we talking about?"

"Charlie."

"Yeah, Charlie. Me and Charlie, we go way back. Now, that's a guy that works the jobs. You know what I'm talking about?"

"Heists."

He winked. "That's why you're a detective."

I pulled a pad of paper closer and grabbed a pen.

Remo motioned toward me. "Let me know if you need me to repeat anything."

"I'm good."

"Yeah, okay. So, Charlie says they need a lookout for a job. The guy they normally use has come down with some sort of gut problem. Irritable bowels or something. That sounds made up, but what do I know? I'm not a doctor. Anyway, the job can't go off without a lookout."

"Understandable."

"And let's be honest, being a lookout sounds like a pretty sweet gig. Stand around. Don't touch nothin'. Keep your eyes open. Watch for the cops and such. So, I said yes."

"What'd you heist?"

Remo leaned forward. "Like confession, right?"

"I promise."

"Good, good." He mimed the sign of the cross but only did the horizon movements before kissing his fingers. I wondered if he'd ever been inside a church. "We knocked over that payday loan joint. You know the one across the street from the Donut Parade?"

My eyes flicked to the newspaper. The article concerning the robbery of Every Day is Pay Day was on the front page. I grabbed the paper.

"It was a sweet deal," Remo said. His voice grew louder as if trying to hold my attention.

I reread the article as he continued to speak. The business was hit a few minutes before closing time—ten p.m.

"Nobody got hurt—" Remo said.

Three men entered the rear of the building. There was no mention of a lookout or a getaway vehicle.

"—but that's because everybody played ball."

I looked up. "Say again?"

"Everybody played ball."

"How so?"

Remo cocked his head. "Confession?"

"Yeah, yeah. Three Hail Marys. Get on with it."

"The owner of the joint was in on it. Smart, huh?" He tapped his temple. "That's what Charlie told me from the beginning. I don't think he was supposed to, but he wanted to make sure I knew everything was good to go. That I had nothing to worry about. There would be no shooting, nobody would call the cops, and everything would be easy as pie."

I tapped the article. "The paper said—"

His eyes widened. "We made the paper?"

"—that you guys took the security tapes."

Remo shrugged. "From what Charlie told me, the Pay Day owner stopped recording before we ever even got there. He had the tapes out and ready to go. Bing-bang-boom. It was fast."

"How fast?"

"I don't know. Couple minutes."

"The paper reported they lost over three hundred thousand." I showed him the newspaper.

Remo laughed. "That's bullshit. Complete and utter. The guy lost about a hundred grand. He's reporting that much for the insurance company."

"So that's what this is—an insurance swindle."

"The guys went in and took the money. The owner gets fifty percent of it back, and we get our fifty."

"How much did you make?"

"Little less than fifty thousand."

"No, you personally."

Remo's face soured. "I was supposed to make ten percent."

"Which was?"

"Forty-eight hundred."

"Not bad for a couple minutes of work."

Remo nodded. "If I got paid."

"What happened?"

"I fucked up."

"How so?"

Remo stood. "Mind if I stand?" He started pacing. "I was on the back. That's where I was supposed to be on the lookout."

"Why the back?"

"Because that's where the entrance is. Oh, right, you wouldn't know that. The front of the building faces the street, so the back door is the entry. Make sense? Anyway, this girl walked by. I should say woman because she wasn't a kid, but she was younger than me. Real pretty thing. She had this video camera—one of those small, handheld ones. You know what I'm talking about?" His hand formed a C, and he held it near his face. "Although she didn't hold it there. She held it like this." His hand—still in the shape of a C—dropped to his chest. "It sounded like she was making a documentary or something. I heard her say, 'Starbucks is down that-a-way, and my favorite store is over there.' Anyway, when she walked by, she saw me and said, 'Hello.'"

"She walked through the back?"

"Through the parking lot, yeah."

"And she pointed the camera at you?"

Remo nodded. "It went everywhere she looked."

"And she still held it at her chest level?"

"Weird, right?"

"What did you do?"

He shrugged a single shoulder. "I didn't want to be rude."

"Of course not."

"I said hello."

"Ah."

"I mean, she was pretty and all." Remo waggled his hand. "She dressed sort of sloppy, but pretty girls can get away with that. You or me, we'd look like bums, but not her. She asked if I lived at the payday loan place, and I said no. I mean, who lives in a building like that? Then she asked if I liked living in Spokane, which is a weird thing to ask a stranger, don't you think?"

"What did you tell her?"

Remo dropped back into his chair. "I said, 'It's the best.' I don't really feel that way since Spokane kinda sucks ass, but I didn't know who she was making the video for. I didn't want my face forever associated with saying something like that even if it is true."

"Smart."

"I thought so." Remo shook his head in disbelief. "Yeah, anyway, we chatted for like half a second, then she went on her way. A minute later, the guys came out, and we took off."

"And you told them about the woman?"

Remo scrunched his nose. "Not right away, no, but eventually, yeah. I guess I didn't really have to, and maybe everything would have been cool if I kept my mouth shut, but we were at Double G's warehouse—"

"Who?"

"Double G. It was his job."

"Why's he called Double G?"

Remo shrugged. "Maybe because he's got a couple grand? I don't know. He's the boss, and nobody fucks with Double G. The dude is kind of scary. Ask anybody. So, there we were—"

"In the warehouse."

"That's right. We were in Double G's warehouse, and everyone was talking about how the robbery went down smooth as ice when Double G turned to me and asked, 'What about you, Remo?' Just like that. 'What about you, Remo?'" He lowered his voice. "'Anything exciting happen while the boys were inside?' And like a dumbass, I told him about the documentary lady." Remo threw his arms into the air. "Why did I do that? Everything unraveled after then."

"How so?"

"They gave me the third degree."

"They?"

Remo waved his hand. "Double G's got this guy— Trace—a real asshole. He's the type of jerk in high school who gave smaller guys swirlies. Remember them? Head in the toilet. Gross, right? Anyway, Trace is one of those guys, but all grown up. He thumped me pretty good for the documentary lady. They kept asking questions like 'what did she look like' and 'where did she go.' You get what I'm saying? I won't lie to you, I thought I might have been at the end of my days right then and there. But when Double G got everything out of me, he told Trace to throw me out. He said he'd better never hear my name again."

I looked at my mostly blank notepad. "Why are you here, Remo?"

"He didn't pay me."

"You said that."

"I want my money."

"Are you asking me to collect? Because I don't do that. Especially if he's as upset as you describe, and there's no way I'm going to strong-arm the guy—that's robbery."

Remo waved his hands. "That's not what I'm saying. I'm not saying that at all."

"What are you saying?"

He leaned forward. "What if I hire you to find the woman—the documentary lady? And you get her to, you know, delete the interview with me. Then the problem with Double G goes away." He kissed the fingers of both hands then opened them quickly. "Poof."

"I don't know."

"What's not to know? The heist came off without a hitch. The other guys got their money. I should get mine, too. I can't help it if I'm nice to pretty girls."

I rubbed my face while I thought. I'd worked in some gray areas before but this one was damn near charcoal. If I was to help, there were two things I needed to know before I started.

"What's my fee?"

Remo shrugged. "I don't know. I'm thinking maybe ten percent?"

"I want half."

"Of $4,800?" His eyes widened. "You're kidding. That's highway robbery."

"Right now, you've got zero. You're asking me to stick my neck out in a way I don't feel comfortable with. If I'm going to do that, and I'm not saying I'm doing that yet, I want a significant carrot."

"What's the other thing?"

"I want to talk with Double G."

He came out of his seat. "What about?" he whined.

"You."

"Me?" the whine worsened. "What for?

"I'm not sticking my neck out for you if this guy will refuse to pay in the end."

Remo dropped into his chair. "He'll pay," he said dejectedly.

"How do you know?"

He half-heartedly raised his hands. "I guess he'll pay."

"If Double G says he'll pay, *and* you agree to fifty percent, I'll take the job."

Remo lowered his head. "Yeah, fine. Fifty percent."

I grabbed my pen. "Now, let's get some facts down. Tell me about this woman again."

***

Eight Ball Billiards sat on the corner of First Avenue and Monroe Street. Neon signs for various beer companies filled the windows. They were illuminated, but the sunshine rendered them almost useless.

I entered the bar and was greeted by the cacophony of people laughing, pool balls clacking, and Ringo Starr's "It Don't Come Easy" playing overhead through hanging speakers.

The bartender turned my way and lifted his chin. I pointed toward the back, and he nodded.

It was busier than I would have expected, but that's how things went in downtown. Some days a bar might be empty around lunchtime, while on other days, it could be nearly packed. Maybe a convention was in town. Or some company retreat was in one of the nearby hotels. But there wasn't a regional event to point to for the burst of interest in billiards.

There were five pool tables. Four were filled with what appeared to be amateurs. I passed them by without so much as an additional glance. The fat man I wanted to see was seated on a bench at the back of the establishment. The pool table near Deacon was empty—it always remained at the ready for him to play. He clutched a pool stick in his hand and looked like a low-end despot. He wore slacks and an oversized purple sweatshirt with the logo of the University of Washington.

As I neared, two men stepped from the shadows. Keith and Mack weren't making an aggressive move. It was simply a reminder that they were there. I motioned to both, and they each went about their business of guarding Deacon.

I sat next to the heavyset man. His attention seemed to be on the newcomers at the billiard tables.

"Is there an event going on?" I asked.

"Church group. Some singles thing. They're meeting for a meal or some such."

Now, I watched the folks at the tables. They seemed to be having a nice time together. I was torn between envy and disdain.

Deacon eyed me. "Did you come by to play a game?"

"Not today."

He swirled his pool stick. "You could use the practice."

I chuckled. "I only need to know if you've heard a name—Double G."

Deacon's face hardened. "Cutler, tell me you're not messing around with Gary Gaspar."

"A guy came to me who needed some help. He's gotten sideways with the man."

"Let that client be." Deacon waggled the stick now. "Gaspar's not a man to trifle with."

"Why's that?"

"How to put this?"

While Deacon thought, I took a moment to study him. He appeared to have lost some weight, but I might have been wrong. Since I met him a couple of years ago, he'd always been obese. That didn't stop him from doing what he was good at—playing pool and trading information. I'm not sure how he made a living doing those two things, but he obviously did well enough to afford a couple of guys as security.

Something seemed off about him, though. I knew better than to ask. One didn't do that with Deacon.

He eyed me. "Gaspar is good at certain things. He pulls heists, insurance scams, you name it. He'll put people together, and the jobs come off. I'll give the man credit for that."

"What's he not good at?"

"Maintaining a crew. He looks at people like a renewable resource."

"Sounds like he needs a Human Resources manager."

Deacon lifted an eyebrow. I thought for sure he would have smiled.

"Be careful of Gaspar," I said. "I got it. He's dangerous."

"Everyone down here is dangerous, Cutler. How badly depends upon the circumstances and opportunity presented. You should know that by now."

***

Double G owned a small warehouse off the corner of

Freya Street and Riverside Avenue. The door to the building was locked. I banged on the door with my fist. A moment later, a latch slid back, and the door opened. A wide-shouldered guy with thick black hair stood there.

"Yeah?"

"I'd like to speak with Double G."

"Nobody here by that name."

"Tell him it's about Remo Lightly."

The big man's lip curled. "Wait."

The door slammed shut, and the latch slid back into place. I walked to the sidewalk and waited. It was about noon now, and the sun hovered overhead in a clear blue sky. It was a comfortable mid-May afternoon. This was my fourth year in Spokane, and I much preferred this weather over Seattle's. The winters tended to be harsher with the cold and snow, but the other seasons were far superior.

Behind me, the latch slid noisily back, and the warehouse's door opened. The big man waved me over. Once I neared, the guy asked, "You carrying?"

"No."

"I gotta check."

"I understand."

He stepped aside, and I entered. The big guy immediately shoved me against the nearest wall and kicked my feet apart. A hand rested on my shoulder.

I looked back at him. "Take it easy on a girl," I said. "This being our first date and all."

"Don't move." His hands roughly ran my length. He checked everywhere, even underneath my groin. When he finished, he pulled my wallet from a back pocket. "All right."

I turned around. "That was thorough."

"This way." He jerked his head for me to follow.

The warehouse had two small offices. The rest of it

appeared to be wide open and filled with a strange assortment of items—a Volkswagen Beetle, a Lotus Esprit, lots of home furnishings, some small construction equipment, and several pinball machines.

"What is all that stuff?" I asked.

"Collateral." The big man stopped at the first office and pointed inside.

Gary Gaspar sat behind a large desk made of dark wood. Nothing was on the surface but a pad of paper, a pen, and a cell phone. On the walls were several framed pieces of abstract art.

Two chairs sat in front of the desk.

"Please," Gaspar said and motioned toward one of the chairs. He was a thin man with closely cropped hair. He was roughly fifty years old with clean skin and alert eyes. On the middle finger of his left hand was a gawdy silver ring.

I sat in the nearest chair.

The big man stepped over to the desk and tossed the wallet onto its surface. He then moved behind me.

"Thank you, Trace," Gaspar said. He removed my driver's license from the wallet. "John Cutler. Name doesn't ring a bell." The thin man looked past my shoulder to his security man. "You neither? Huh." His gaze returned to me. "Okay, Cutler. You want to talk about Remo Lightly. This better be good."

"He came to me."

Gaspar pointed at his desk. "Was he the one who told you how to find me?" His face hardened.

"Your reputation precedes you, Gary."

Something hit the back of my head, and I flinched. I glanced back at Trace.

The big man's lip curled. "It's Double G."

"Easy, Trace," Gaspar said. "I think Cutler here was making a point about my reputation."

I faced forward.

"Isn't that what you were doing, Cutler? Saying you could have found me without the help of Remo."

"I was."

Gasper crossed his arms. "My reputation is something I've worked to cultivate. You know what that word means?"

I wanted to say something snarky, but I simply nodded. I didn't want another smack.

Double G pulled his left hand free from the crook of the right elbow. He held up the middle finger and showed me the gawdy ring. "You see this? It's a Super Bowl ring. No bullshit." He extended his hand toward me. "Super Bowl Twenty-seven. Cowboys and the Bills. Terrible game, but I made a loan to this second-string lineman who you probably never heard of." He tapped the side of the ring with his thumb. "There's his last name. Ring a bell? Didn't think so. Still, the guy was on the team. Lived up in Nine Mile after he left the game. Guy thought he could jerk me around on paying what he owed. What do you think he wishes for now?"

I didn't answer.

"He wishes he could walk without a limp," Trace said.

"Exactly." Gaspar knocked the ring on the desk. "Exactly."

I wondered if they had rehearsed that routine before.

Double G recrossed his arms. "So, now you know the kind of man I am. What kind of man are you, Cutler? Let's find out. You came down here for Remo. Why would a man like you do such a thing?"

"He asked me to find something."

"And what would that be?"

"A video."

Gaspar's head tilted somewhat. If he were playing poker, it would have been only the slightest of tells, but I could see he wasn't pleased with my statement.

"So we're on the same page," Gaspar said, "look at Trace."

I glanced back. The security man now pointed a gun at my head. He didn't show any emotion.

"So, you see, Cutler—"

I faced Gaspar.

"—that you better choose your next words very carefully. Because if you're thinking about shaking me down, it's not going to go well."

"That's not what this is about. He asked me to find a video—"

"Which means he told you about a job." Gaspar angrily shook his head. "Remo told you how to find me, then he tells you about a job he had no business being a part of."

I started to open my mouth, but Gaspar slammed his fist on the desk.

"Remo's dead!"

From behind me, Trace said, "I'll take care of it."

I lifted a hand. "Wait."

This whole thing had turned into a mess. I'd only wanted to clear things up, and now I'd put Remo Lightly in the crosshairs of Double G.

Gaspar stood. "My day was going pretty well until you walked in here and fucked it all up."

"I'll take care of it," Trace said.

"You're damn right, you will."

"I can find the video," I said firmly.

My words and tone interrupted their conversation, and they stopped talking. I had no idea if I could truly deliver the video but being talked about like a cow awaiting slaughter pissed me off. I slowly stood and turned so I could see them both.

Trace still pointed his gun at my head. He was too far

away for me to try anything but to simply reason with him. "That's unnecessary."

"I'll decide what's unnecessary for Trace," Gaspar said. "What makes you think you can find the video?"

"There's a business card in that wallet. It's with the cash."

Gaspar grabbed the billfold and opened it. He flipped through the money and pulled out a slightly wrinkled business card. "Private detective. Great." He tossed the wallet back to the desk. "Remo told a private dick about the job. This gets better every minute."

"I keep telling you, Remo came to me to find the video."

Gaspar lifted an eyebrow. "He hired you?"

"I haven't agreed to it yet. I wanted to talk with you first."

"What for?"

"To make sure Remo could pay me."

Now, Gaspar spun the business card onto the desk. "Good luck. The guy doesn't have two nickels to rub together."

"That's what I figured, but you owe him forty-eight hundred."

"I owe him shit." Gaspar's brow furrowed. "This sounds vaguely close to a shakedown."

"I promise, it's not."

Double G looked at his security man. "I know a shakedown when I hear one. How about you?"

Trace inched forward.

Gaspar pointed at the big man. "If you shoot him in here, you gotta clean it up."

"Not a problem."

"I'm talking wiping everything down, not just getting rid of the body. Like bleaching the fuck out of this place. You understand that?"

Frustration crossed Trace's face. "I get it. Totally. Can I shoot him now or what?"

I lifted my hands further into the air. "I get why you held Remo's fee."

Gaspar's attention returned to me.

"It makes perfect sense," I said. "I mean, truly. But if I understand it, the job went off with only that small hitch—a video."

Gaspar's eyes flicked to Trace then back to me. He reached out and gently pushed down the security man's arms. The gun moved away from my face.

Double G said, "I will neither confirm nor deny your accusation."

I lowered my arms to shoulder height. "Remo let that video happen, but he wants to make it right by hiring me. What I'm asking is, if I bring it to you, will you make good on his portion of the job? Otherwise, he won't have the money to pay me. Why should I bust my hump for no fee?"

Gaspar seemed to consider my question. "What's Remo paying you?"

"Half."

"Of his fee?" He seemed surprised for a moment, then burst into laughter. "No wonder you came here with your balls out. You're a motivated sumbitch. What if there's not a pot of gold at the end of the rainbow? What if I decide not to pay?"

"Then I'll stay home. Maybe count the flowers on the wall."

Gaspar shook his head. "That doesn't work for me."

"How so?"

"I got all the leverage here. I know who you are, where you work. You wanna live so you'll do the job—for *free*."

"I made a mistake coming here."

"Ya think?" Double G grinned. "But that doesn't change your reality."

"There's no way I'm working for free."

Trace lifted his gun again, and my head instinctively moved away. He was still too far away for me to make a move on him.

"You might want to rechoose your words," Gaspar said.

"Here's the situation. You can force me to do the job without compensation. I'll agree to that and walk out of here. Then I'm going to walk home and become a problem. Who knows what I do when I get there? Maybe I get my gun and come right back. Or maybe I call the cops."

"I'd advise against both of those," Gaspar said.

Trace moved closer towards his boss. "Let me do him right now."

"Hold on. We're talking."

"He's threatening us," Trace said.

I ignored the security man. "But if you promise to pay Remo, I'll get my fee when I deliver the video. I'll be a very productive beaver."

Gaspar studied me for a moment. He turned his head slightly toward Trace. "What do you think?"

"I think we should shoot him and Remo both. Let's not waste any more time."

Double G set his hand on Trace's arm and once again pushed down the gun. "There'll be plenty of time for that." He walked behind his desk and sat. "Especially if Cutler fails to deliver a video. Isn't that right?"

I shrugged.

"All right," Gaspar said. "You got yourself a deal. Find that video, bring it to me, and I'll pay Remo. But if you don't—"

He didn't need to finish the threat. I had it memorized.

Every Day is Pay Day was located on the southeast corner of Hamilton Street and Illinois Avenue. It was in an older, single-story building. It appeared to have once been a gas station. The pumps had been removed, but the canopy remained. Several cars were parked underneath it.

When I asked Remo during our meeting to describe the woman who videotaped him, it took a series of prompts to get anywhere.

"Did she say her name?" I asked.

Remo shrugged. "No, but we didn't talk that long. It was maybe a couple minutes if anything."

"What color was she?"

"White."

I jotted notes onto my pad as we went. "How old was she?"

"I don't know. Late twenties, I guess. Younger than you, for sure. No offense. That makes her a helluva lot younger than me."

"You said she dressed sloppily?"

Remo rubbed his chin. "Yeah, you know. Frumpy but like on purpose. The way smart people do to show they aren't into fashion. Which I think is stupid because she was pretty."

"But frumpy."

"Her clothes were frumpy, but not her. Does that make sense?"

"What color was her hair?"

"Black." Remo's head bobbled from side to side. "Well, brown maybe. Dark brown. No, probably black. It was dark out, and the parking lot lights were on. Remember when you were a kid, and you had to go home when the streetlights came on?

"You realized she was sort of pretty by the parking lot lights?"

"Now that you say it, it sounds kind of romantic, huh? Maybe I'll end up in that paper's I Saw You section. Wouldn't that be cool if she wanted to find me?"

"Did she say anything about where she lived?"

Remo's brow furrowed. "Like, did she give me her address? I wish. Although…"

"What?"

"She did say she was going for a soda. She said she did that every night. I thought that was cute. Who drinks soda anyway? I guess kids do, but—"

"Did she say where she was going?"

"To get a soda. I just said."

I stared at him.

"Oh," Remo said, "I see. No, she didn't say, but there's a convenience store up the way."

"Which way? North or south?"

"It's to the south."

"So, she came from the north?"

"Right, right. She came from the north."

"And you were standing at the back of the building?"

"That's right."

"So she cut through the parking lot."

Remo nodded. "Off that side street. I can't remember its name."

It was Illinois Avenue like in the Monopoly game. The woman with the camera had cut through the parking lot before heading southbound on Hamilton Street. I stopped briefly at the payday loan business to get my bearings, and then I continued southbound to find the convenience store.

There was a gas station at the corner of Hamilton and Baldwin.

I pulled into the store's parking lot and backed into a

parking spot so I could see the convenience store's entrance. It was a long shot. I knew it before I came, but what other choice did I have? The probability of finding the woman was slim—minuscule, at best. It felt like my odds of success were as good as what?

Finding a needle in a haystack. Yeah, probably.

I leaned my head back and watched a dusty Ford pickup sidle up to a gas pump. Its owner climbed out and trotted into the store.

Who puts a needle in a haystack anyway? What a stupid idiom.

The pickup owner left the store, walked back to his truck, and climbed in. He drove away.

How about finding a virgin in a whorehouse? It was a crude saying, but it held a truth that the haystack didn't. I liked it better but couldn't remember if I'd ever been in a whorehouse when I was a cop.

My fingers drummed along the steering wheel as several other customers entered then left.

What about finding an honest man in Congress? A smile spread across my lips. Yeah. I liked that idiom the best. That felt more hopeless than the needle or the virgin.

I chuckled to myself. Then I felt stupid for doing so— a grown man, giggling in his truck.

A woman walked into the parking lot. She was a fashion mess. She wore an oversized cashmere sweater that hung unbuttoned. Her baggy t-shirt displayed the grimacing face of Tupac Shakur. Her plaid shorts hung below her knees, and she wore red Converse without socks. Her dark hair hung to her shoulders.

She carried a handheld video camera at her chest and talked while she walked. The woman waved her arm and pointed as she went. When she stepped up to the store's sidewalk, she stopped talking, lowered her camera, and entered the building.

While she was inside, I decided not to confront her in the parking lot. I wasn't worried about witnesses or the store's cameras. I wasn't going to do anything illegal. If the woman didn't want to give me the videotape, I wasn't going to take it. I'd already made peace with that.

But I wanted to know where she lived. I thought I might have more success talking with her at her home.

A few minutes later, the woman exited with a large soda in one hand and the camera in the other. She immediately lifted the camera to her chest and started filming again.

Her gait was mostly shuffling. This was due to her attention being divided by the sipping of soda along with the almost constant narration she provided during her walk. I stayed where I was until she was almost out of sight. Then I left the parking lot, drove a couple of double blocks north on Hamilton, and pulled into the parking lot of Every Day is Pay Day. I popped out onto Illinois and came to the stop sign.

Several moments passed before I realized she was headed right toward me. The camera held at her chest would no doubt pick up my truck. Even though I wasn't doing anything illegal, my sitting there waiting would look suspicious. She was still a block away, but if I stayed where I was, she'd notice me sooner or later.

I turned north and looped the block but continued south so that I could come up behind her. I stopped at the corner of Ermina and Hamilton.

The woman continued sipping and narrating while she shuffled along. By now, she'd cut through the parking lot of Every Day is Pay Day, and I lost sight of her.

When there was a break in traffic, I turned north and hurried back to Illinois Avenue. When I turned eastbound onto that block, I saw her several houses down the street.

The woman ascended a small set of stairs, balanced her soda in the crook of the arm holding the camera, and entered the house.

I parked and got out.

The house was a small yellow affair with white trim. Even in the darkness of early evening, I could tell the house needed painting and a new roof. The lawn was dry, and the flowers along the front of the house were barren. A small black mailbox hung near the front door. Black and gold lettering announced the name of the homeowner as *Holt*.

I knocked.

A moment later, the door opened, and a woman in her sixties eyed me with curiosity. "Yes?"

"I'm sorry to bother you this late at night, ma'am. My name is John Cutler. There was a woman that came up here. She had a video camera."

"My daughter, Laura. Yes."

"May I speak with her? There was an accident up the street, and I'm hoping she might have recorded it."

The woman frowned before looking over her shoulder. When she faced me again, she said, "I'm sorry, but it's not going to do any good."

"Why not?"

"There's nothing in the camera."

"Excuse me?"

Her smile was apologetic. "Laura had an accident many years ago. Very severe. She fell while mountain biking, and the result..." The woman's face softened further. "Well, she carries that camera with her everywhere now. None of us know why. The darn thing hasn't worked in years. But for whatever reason, it makes her happy. Who am I to tell her to stop doing that?"

Laura approached from behind her mother. She still carried the soda, and the camera was held near her chest.

"Who are you?"

"I'm John Cutler," I said.

The younger woman pointed the camera at me. "What do you do?"

"I drive a truck." I didn't want to say I was a private investigator for many reasons.

She slurped on her soda.

"I like your camera," I said.

"Thank you." She lifted it higher. "I'm making a movie."

"I can see that."

"Smile."

I did.

"It's about the city. Do you live here?"

"I do."

"Do you like it?"

"I do."

"Me, too." Laura turned and walked away.

The mother eyed me, "So, you see? There'll be no video of the accident."

"She's okay walking around? I don't mean to be rude, but it's after ten, and there's traffic."

By the look on the mother's face, I could see I had crossed a line.

"I'm sorry," I said. "She's an attractive woman, and someone might try to harm her."

The mother glanced to make sure her daughter hadn't returned. "Laura's allowed to go the store and back. That's all. She goes three or four times a day. I call them when she leaves the house. They call me when she leaves the store. Laura has an account there that I bring current every week. It gives her a sense of freedom. I don't know if that makes a difference, but it allows me to remember who she used to be. I hope it allows her that, too."

I stepped back from the door. "I'm sorry for bothering

you."

"No bother," the woman said. "And good luck with
your accident."

***

The next morning, I was back in Double G's office.
Once again, Gary sat in his chair, and Trace stood behind
me. I hated the setup, but I expected nothing less.

"There's no video," I said.

Gaspar leaned back in his chair. "The fuck does that
mean, Cutler?"

"It means the woman who took it is brain-damaged." I
tapped the side of my head. "She had an accident a few
years ago. Now she carries around a broken camera
pretending to make movies."

He studied me. "You're jerking my chain."

I told him the whole story then. How I found her, what
the mother said, and my interaction with Laura Holt. I left
out her name and her address, but he got the complete
picture.

Gaspar pinched his nose while he thought. When he
came to something, he laughed. He looked at Trace.
"Wouldn't you know it? Remo chats up some retarded
bitch and causes us all a bunch of heartburn. Who was it
that suggested we let him in the job?"

"Charlie," Trace said.

"Well, Charlie's retarded, too. Why the fuck are we
working with him?"

"The times," Trace said.

"The times," Gaspar agreed. His gaze returned to me.
"Now we got us a decision. What to do with you."

"You pay me," I said.

"What's stopping Trace from popping you right where
you sit and saving me forty-eight large?"

"Nothing," the security man said.

I asked, "You ever play pool with a guy named Deacon?"

"The fat man?" Gaspar crossed his arms. "No. Why?"

"I play with him, and he knows I'm meeting with you right now."

"Is that supposed to scare me?"

I leaned forward. "He owes me a favor."

Gaspar's face flattened. "Christ, Cutler. I was only fucking around. I'm gonna pay. Relax, will ya?"

We stared at each other for a few moments.

"But I'm not paying you," Gaspar said. "My debt is with Remo. I pay him, and he pays you. That's how polite society works."

"When have you ever been polite?"

Something cracked against the back of my head.

"Trace takes offense to that," Gaspar said. "Me, too."

I rubbed the stinging as I stood. "I apologize. It was uncalled for."

"But not untrue." Gaspar stood and extended his hand. "Send Deacon my regards."

***

A couple of days passed, and Remo Lightly still hadn't returned my calls. I finally got worried that maybe Double G didn't pay him and instead sent his goon.

I stopped by Remo's apartment around lunchtime. He lived in the basement of a converted house in the Perry District. I knocked, but there was no answer. A woman came around the corner. She was in her early fifties with platinum hair and the rosy glow of a heavy drinker. She was slightly overweight with large breasts that almost spilled out of her low-cut pink t-shirt. It featured the honest tagline *Yours for the Taking*.

"He's gone," she said.

"Remo?"

She wriggled her butt, then smacked her hands and pushed one into the air. "Like a bat out of hell strapped to a rocket."

"When was this?"

"Couple days ago."

"Any reason why?"

The woman moved closer and grabbed onto a support column to steady herself. It looked and smelled as if she'd already done some heavy drinking that morning. Her watery eyes blinked slowly, and her nose scrunched as if she was trying to bring me into focus. "What'd you say?"

"Remo. He left in a hurry?"

"That's right. Some big fella came by. You know those types with no necks. This one reminded me of my husband—the first one, the handsome bastard. Boy, I made a mistake there."

So, Double G had sent Trace. Maybe he put a scare into Remo, and the guy fled town out of fear.

"I saw them talking over there." The woman pointed toward the sidewalk. "The big fella gave Remo an envelope then left."

"How big was it?"

"Like the thing you send mail in." She mimed the size with her fingers then quickly held onto the column again for support. "You got bills, don't ya? In an envelope like that."

I frowned.

"Well, hell, you shoulda seen Remo. The way he whooped and hollered, you woulda thought he won the lottery or something. He even hugged me, the stupid bastard, like he's got a shot at this." Her watery eyes took me in then. "What'd you say your name was?"

"What happened then?"

She blinked slowly. Then her eyes widened suddenly, and she jerked back. She shook her head and once again took me in.

"What happened then?" I repeated.

"With what?"

"Remo," I said.

She curled her lip. "Him." She waved angrily. "Dumb bastard went into his apartment for an hour or two." Her eyes rolled up. "Maybe it was fifteen minutes. I dunno. Normally, he's pretty quiet, but I heard a lot of banging down there. When he came out, I was sitting right over there—" She pointed to the front steps. "—smoking a cigarette. Remo had a couple of bags with him and he said he was out of here." She jerked a thumb over her shoulder. "He even said he called the landlord and told him to kiss his ass." The woman howled with laughter. "Kiss his ass. Can you believe that? I'd never have the nuts to do that."

Anger swelled in my chest.

"You lookin' for a place to rent?" She pointed to Remo's apartment. "It's a nice place, and I live right around the back." She crooked a finger and made a circular motion. "You could come over for a cup of sugar any time."

"Did he say where he was going?"

Her face soured, and she pursed her lips. "You're sure hung up on Remo. You two weren't boyfriends or nothing, were you?"

"He owed me money."

The woman eyed me. "You got money?"

"Where did he go?"

She sighed. "Remo, Remo, Remo. All you care about is Remo!" She swayed. "He told me not to tell, but I'll tell you since we're gonna be neighbors. Besides, I'm sort of jealous of where he went."

I wanted to yell. I wanted to punch something. I waved my hand at the drunk woman. "Never mind."

"Don't you wanna know?"

"Keep it to yourself."

She laughed. "I probably woulda gone with the goofy bastard if he'da asked."

I climbed into my truck and started it.

The woman couldn't be heard over the revving of my truck's engine, but it sure as hell looked as if she shouted that Remo went to Mexico.

Notes

Thank you for reading *Cutler's Cases*.

Four of the short stories were originally written around the time I first wrote the first three novels (roughly 2004-2007). One of the short stories was published, but the other three were dumped into a digital drawer along with the novels. As I mentioned in the Introduction, the stories originally featured a character named Jack Collins.

Nothing happened with these short stories until John Cutler was born. When that happened, new life was breathed into everything. I found the character's voice and am incredibly proud of the tales you now hold.

Let me share a little about each one.

MANNY

"Manny" has remained my favorite of the four original John Cutler short stories. I've liked it for several reasons.

First, the fight in the opening scene was fast and brutal. The fact that Cutler lost adds to its realism.

Next, Delores went to Cutler for help, not because of a referral or because she read about him in the newspaper. Instead, she chose him because of proximity—they lived in the same neighborhood. How many of our choices in life are simply dictated by convenience?

And lastly, Manny wasn't running around on his woman but was instead collecting debts because he needed money to help his mother-in-law. I liked that twist.

Of the four stories I wrote a decade and a half ago, it's the one that changed the least. It needed some cleaning, but nothing in the story made me wince.

THE PROBLEM WITH SUZIE

I originally wrote "The Problem with Suzie" after hearing Marcia Ball sing "Another Man's Woman" on the album *Safe House*. It's a companion piece to Andrew Vachss' novel of the same name.

The problem with the original version of the story was Jack Collins. He was too tough, a smart-mouthed jerk, and he tried to woo the female cop at the end of the story. It all felt wrong.

Even back then, I knew there was something not right about it. But I wasn't sure how to fix it. A young writer is too afraid to throw away words that they've written. They cling to those paragraphs like precious gems.

When Cutler was born, the story was heavily cut and rewritten.

Cutler's still a guy that makes mistakes, but he doesn't have to be an idiot about everything.

ECHOES OF HER

"Echoes of Her" is the continuation of Cutler's love story with Paige McIntyre. She's the woman he fell for which led to his eventual termination from the Seattle Police Department. In *Cutler's Return*, he goes to her aid, but she winds up murdered before Cutler can figure out what is really going on.

When I originally wrote the first three novels and the short stories, Paige played a much larger role. She was an albatross that hung around Jack Collins' neck. He couldn't move on with his life because of it.

Looking back at those first drafts, the Paige impact was too melodramatic. It was like a cheesy soap opera. Beyond that, there was no growth in Cutler since he couldn't get beyond her. As I rewrote the short stories along with books two and three, I downplayed Paige's memory. I removed her from all the short stories (except this one) and even the third book. While Jack Collins couldn't move on, John Cutler needed to.

However, I didn't want Cutler to forget his roots. Could a man truly forget a woman he compromised himself for? No. There was no way Cutler could ever get Paige fully out of his system, no matter how much he repressed his feelings.

I didn't change the critical link between Mia's resemblance to Paige. Beyond that, most of the story was rewritten to align with John Cutler's history.

It's a much better tale.

SISTER WIVES

"Sister Wives" was first published as "The Big Blonde" in *The Ex-Factor*.

The story idea and title came from a Mickey Spillane paperback, *Me, Hood!* The cover for that book features a drawing of a striking woman with long blond hair. I imagined her being very tall. I loved the image the first time I saw it.

I cringe when I read the original version of this story now.

Thank God that Cutler came along. I toned down the tough-guy talk from Jack Collins. I also pulled back all of Jack's dog-in-heat behavior. That stuff bugs me now. I hate when I read it in others' work, and I'm surprised so much of it existed in my early stuff. It showed how immature I was in my writing then.

Everyone should grow—even writers.

I also changed the title of the story. When I first wrote it, the title was an homage to those tales of yesteryear like *The Big Sleep*. Two things have changed since I wrote.

First, I grew to dislike the tough-talking private eyes that I based the earlier version of this story on. Second, society changed, and the idea of naming a story, "The Big Blonde," no longer held appeal to me. I scrapped that title and moved on.

REMO LIGHTLY

This is the newest story in the collection, and I struggled for a title.

While I was writing the fifth Cutler novel, I realized I didn't have a strong enough understanding of Cutler's relationship with a couple of characters—Remo Lightly and Double G. So I stopped what I was doing and wrote this story.

It was a fun exercise and worked out wonderfully. Not only was the Remo character a joy to write, but I liked the conclusion of the story. Cutler takes the job with some trepidation and then is screwed for it in the end. It seemed almost poetic.

That's what I like about Cutler. Things don't often work out for him in nice, neat ways. This was an opportunity to show that when John Cutler wins, he can still lose.

Thanks for reading. I'll see you down the road as Cutler continues his adventures.

Colin Conway
Spring 2022

Did You Enjoy the Book?

Thank you for reading *Cutler's Cases*. I'm always grateful when a reader takes time out of their day to comment on one of my novels. If you do write a review, please email me and let me know. I'd love to say thanks!

About the Author

Colin Conway is the creator of the 509 Crime Stories, a series of novels set in Eastern Washington with revolving lead characters. They are standalone tales and can be read in any order.

He also created the Cozy Up series which pushes the envelope of the cozy genre. Libby Klein, author of the Poppy McAllister series, says *Cozy Up to Death* is "Not your grandma's cozy."

Colin co-authored the Charlie-316 series. The first novel in the series, *Charlie-316*, is a political/crime thriller that has been described as "riveting and compulsively readable," "the real deal," and "the ultimate ride-along."

He served in the U.S. Army and later was an officer of the Spokane Police Department. He's owned a laundromat, invested in a bar, and run a karate school. Besides writing crime fiction, he is a commercial real estate broker.

Colin lives with his beautiful girlfriend, three wonderful children, and a codependent Vizsla that rules their world.

www.ingramcontent.com/pod-product-compliance
Lightning Source LLC
Chambersburg PA
CBHW031539310726
48971CB00008B/2549